Past e

MW01166943

Kudzu

Kathleen Walls

Global Authors Publications

Kudzu
©Kathleen Walls 2003

ISBN 0-9728513-9-9
Library of Congress Number 2003107106

First published in 2003 by
Global Authors Publications

*Filling the **GAP** in publishing*

Edited by Kristie Leigh Maguire and Patricia Reames
Cover Art by Kathleen Walls
Interior Design by Kathleen Walls

Printed in USA for Global Authors Publications

Kudzu

To my daughter, Veronica,
my number one fan.

Acknowledgements

Many thanks are in order for the entire gang at Global Authors Publications. They are the greatest bunch of people anywhere.

Many people inspired me to write this book, the crafters who keep the old Appalachian traditions alive in their work, the musicians who still sing and play the old ballads and those historians who record the history of these mountains.

A special thanks to Sam Ensley, a fine local musician who plays many of the old tunes. I needed the words of the song Buffalo Boy. Sam was kind enough to get the version used in this book from some other great mountain musicians, Don and Laeta Smith. They learned the song originally from Betty Smith, one more of the mountain balladeers. That's the way all of the mountain music came down to us. One musician passed it on to another.

Several books were particularly helpful in my research, *The Foxfire Books*, edited by Elliot Wiggington, and *These Storied Mountains* by John Parris.

While I have tried to capture the background and culture of the mountains as accurately as possible, this is a work of fiction and all characters live strictly in my imagination, nowhere else. They bear no intentional resemblance to any person living or dead. Likewise, Bluejay and its businesses and offices do not reflect any actual place

Prologue
March 10, 1879, Bluejay, Georgia

Louisa crept out of her rope bed and down the loft's ladder. She didn't put on her boots until she stood in the moonlight outside the cabin door. Her thoughts tumbled like water in a mountain stream. She had to catch Lillith. She wasn't sure what she could say to her beautiful big sister but she couldn't stand what was going on. She knew Lillith was going to meet Preacher Jonathan at the barn in the hollow between their cabin and the big house on the hill. *It ain't fittin'. I know the preacher is so handsome but he's married. Got a li'l 'un and his wife is al'ays so sick. T'aint right what Lillith was doing sneaking out to sleep with a married man and him a preacher man at that.*

Louisa hurried between the pines and hollyberry that bordered the rock-strewn path. Sprouts of that new plant, Kudzu, which Mr. Stuart had brought back from Philadelphia to control erosion were taking root in the sunny spots near the barn. In the distance, she thought she heard a gunshot. She stopped on the edge of the clearing to gather her thoughts. At that moment, Lillith burst from the ragged opening where once two double doors had stood. She passed within inches of Louisa but didn't see her. *I'll just go on in and talk to Preacher Jonathan. I'll make him see he's doin' wrong. He's got a wife.* A thought crept unbidden into her mind. *If'n his wife died, there's someone else who loves him more'an Lillith ever could. I would make him a fine true wife. Lots of girls marry at thirteen around here.*

When her eyes adjusted to the gloom of the barn, she knew the preacher wouldn't have to worry about woman problems any more. He lay on the straw in the first stall. There was a small hole in the center of his forehead and a pool of blood on the floor.

2002, Bluejay, Georgia

Casey leaned on her shovel and admired her work. It had taken all day. Her auburn hair was flecked with hay from the mulch and her hands were smeared with manure. Her jeans were red at the knees and seat from the Georgia clay. To call her shirt disreputable would have been complementary. She was exhausted but totally self satisfied as she surveyed her new garden. The morning's backbreaking work was worth it. Her garden was planted and if the unseasonable weather continued, she would be feasting on its bounty soon. The manure she had painstakingly hauled in tubs from the Track Gap Stables had darkened the earth to rich brown and the tomato, okra, squash and watermelon seedlings stood like proud toy soldiers.

Movement up the hill at the old Stuart house caught her eye. Rumors around town were rampant. Someone had moved in but no one seemed to know more than that. The huge old farmhouse had been boarded up for several years. Casey had heard that it had once belonged to some distant family connection but she was a bit foggy on just how it fit into the family tree. Someone had purchased it and had been repairing it. Casey suppressed the pang of envy at the thought of someone else acquiring her dream house. As a tiny child, she had stood right here with Granny Weesie and listened to her tell about the people who lived in it now and who had lived in it when Granny was young. Casey couldn't recall a single name now except "Stuart". No point being a dog in the manger, she told herself. Her divorce had left her poor as the proverbial church mouse. She could never afford the Stuart place, even in its present rundown condition.

Suddenly, out of nowhere, two brown and tan explosions of energy erupted from the underbrush directly into her new garden plot. They rolled, romped and trampled until nothing was left standing. "Get! Shoo! Scram, you beasts!" The dogs ignored her and continued the total devastation of her garden.

Nothing she could do seemed to get their attention but when Smokey, her fluffy black cat, moved into their line of vision, they were out of the garden like a shot. Smokey headed up the nearest pine tree. They settled in at the base and began howling and barking as Smokey calmly surveyed his pursuers from the first branch.

At that moment, a man emerged from the path leading uphill to the Stuart Place. "Tater, Snuffy! Quit that racket. Get over here." He had spoken in a low voice but the dogs instantly stopped barking and ran to his side.

He stooped, indulgently rubbing their backs. "Sorry if they upset your kitty, Ma'am."

He looked up at her with the most incredibly blue eyes she had ever seen. When he straightened up, he must have reached at least six feet. His Levi's fit him well and left no doubt of his masculinity, even if his rugged face hadn't proclaimed that same fact. Any other time she might have been impressed with his craggy good looks, but the memory of the hours of tilling, digging, removing the endless rocks, working in the smelly manure, all now wasted effort thanks to his unruly pack of hounds, enraged her. "Those beasts should be on chains! They're vicious!" she exploded. "Look what they did my garden."

"They are not vicious. They're just puppies." He looked down at her with a smile playing around his mouth. "Besides any fool knows you can't plant any of that stuff and expect it to grow. We're sure to have at least one more freeze up here."

"Why you arrogant jackass! You're trespassing on my property and so are those hateful hounds from hell you set loose on my garden! And you dare call me a fool?" She fumbled for threats dire enough, more to repay his insult than his dogs' damages. Ray had always called her names, most of them worse than "fool". She had taken enough of that during her marriage. Ray had always tried to belittle her and make her feel like a stupid "little woman". Now that she was through with her ex-husband, she was never going to let another man put her down. Her emerald eyes flashed a warning fire. "Do you realize I could sue you for damages?"

"Whoa, lady. We're not in Hotlanta. Up here in the mountains, neighbors settle their differences among themselves, not in law courts. I have every intention of repaying you for the damages the pups did. I just wanted to point out it's too early to plant vegetables up here yet."

She was furious and he didn't seem to consider the situation more than an amusing incident, probably something to recount to his hunting buddies next time he and his hounds from hell went out to shoot some poor frightened deer. That, on top of everything else, caused her control to break like a raging flood over a dam. "Well, thank you very much for the weather report. A dumb little gal like me couldn't know if some big, strong man didn't tell her." She let the sarcasm sink in for a moment, then glared at him, "Listen, Bubba, if I want a weather report, I turn on the TV. I don't need any advice from a dumb hillbilly. You probably plant by the signs, too!"

He chuckled, "Matter of fact, I do."

Enough was enough. "Get off my land! Now! Take those... those beasts with you," she screamed.

"Yes, ma'am. Anything to oblige a 'lady'." He sauntered calmly back up the hill.

Casey stomped her foot and threw the shovel she still clutched in her hand to the ground. Stomping in Georgia clay was not too satisfactory and the shovel just fell across her other foot, causing her to howl in pain. Totally frustrated, she marched inside. She filled the old enamel pot with its blue cornflower design and sat it on the eye of her ancient stove. The kettle had been Granny Weesie's, and a cup of tea made in it never failed to soothe her ruffled spirits. Some of her earliest memories were of sitting in this very kitchen with her Granny Weesie and listening to her tales of hidden Confederate gold. Granny had always ended the tales with, "One day I'll tell you where 'tis."

Granny had really been her great-grandmother. She died at a hundred and four. Of course, she had never told her tiny descendant where to hunt for this mysterious treasure. Casey remembered her mother scolding Granny for "filling the child's head with such foolishness."

Granny had always shaken her head and muttered, "Taint foolishness. 'Tis an awful truth 'n I've gotta rid myself of it one day. Little Casey, she's my onlyst hope."

The whistling kettle tore Casey from her reverie. She dunked her tea bag and settled back to enjoy it just as the phone rang.

"Hello?"

"Casey, it's me."

Casey recognized the voice of her cousin and employer, Velma Lou Dyer. In the weeks she had been working as a reporter for Velma Lou's paper, The Bluejay Bugle, she had come to recognize two things: her cousin only called when she wanted something, and Velma Lou didn't want to do any work she could shove off on someone else unless said work involved a lot of prestige or a good looking man. So she knew before the conversation progressed any further that Velma Lou was going to ask her to put in a few more than the fifty plus hours she had already logged in. "Yes, Velma Lou?"

"Darlin', I need a favor. I need you to attend a reception at the Experiment Station and do a teensy weensy little interview afterwards."

"When?"

"Why, right after the reception."

"No, Velma Lou. I mean, when is the reception?"

"Oh, it's tonight, at seven."

"Velma, it's almost six now. I'm a mess. Won't you be there? Can't you do it?"

"Darlin', I'm just going as a guest. I'll be all dressed and don't want to have to mess with the camera and taking notes and all. Besides, I've got a date with Dirk. We're just going to show our faces out of politeness, then we're off to Atlanta for some dinin' and dancin' and whatever. In fact, I probably won't be back until Monday morning so I'll probably be a bit late at the office."

"Okay. I'll do it. Who do I interview?"

"Thanks so much, darlin'. I knew I wouldn't regret hiring you. You need to interview the new supervisor for the Experiment Station. The reception is in his honor. He's a Dr. Leopold Schmidt; he got the appointment because he's an expert on Kudzu, of all things. I'm sure he's just an old fuddy-duddy professor type, but humor him. We need a flattering interview for this week's edition. Oh, and get a picture. Swing by the office and pick up the digital camera so we won't have to worry about developing it."

Casey jumped into a quick shower, wriggled into her sleek teal green dress, slapped on a minimum of makeup and ran a comb through her hair. She hated to have to rush on mountain roads. Driving in the mountains was an exercise for all the senses. It differed each season, sometimes from day to day. The contrast of color was like a kaleidoscope. The red earth, the wildflowers growing along the road and in little crevasses up the mountain sides, the rocks themselves, some gray with little sparkling flecks of mica inside, some gleaming quartz with golden veins through them, and the trees, now varying hues of green interspersed with the flowering dogwoods graced with fragile white blossoms, this was the color of the mountains on a bright spring day. She reveled in the different scents. Fresh mountain air was a combination of grass, pine and other more subtly scented trees, the smell of the water dribbling down the cliffs releasing the mountain's mysterious mineral components. With the window down, she could hear the rushing water as it clamored over the rocks seeking lower ground. She knew if she stopped and ran her fingers through that water, it would be icy cold in spite of the warm sun beaming overhead. All was not perfection, even here in this sparsely inhabited Eden. Casey knew that if she did step off the road to reach that sparkling water, the blackberry brambles would scratch her legs. If she tasted the unripe red berries, they would be bitter. Worse, if she nibbled on the lush looking blue pokeberries, they would poison her. The mountains offered subsistence to those who loved and studied them, but there were hidden pitfalls for any one foolish enough to take on the mountains unprepared.

Driving to retrieve the camera, she had time to reflect on her confrontation with her new neighbor. She was thoroughly ashamed of the stereotypical remarks she had made. After all, the hounds from hell were just puppies and he had offered to pay for the damages. She knew she owed him an apology. Well, tomorrow was Sunday and she would walk up the hill and explain how hot and tired she had been and all the work she had put into the garden as an excuse for her behavior. Of course she wouldn't explain about Ray and his verbal abuse, which made her super sensitive to the slightest derogatory comment. She wouldn't explain about the summers she had spent here with her Great Granny Weesie as a toddler. Granny Weesie would always take her down to the garden to pick fresh tomatoes for her lunch. Then they would go back to the cabin and sit on the porch and eat juicy tomato sandwiches on homemade bread as Granny Weesie would regale her with stories about buried treasure. She was only five when Granny Weesie died, but those early summers still were indelibly engraved in her memory as some of the happiest of her life.

She made a brief stop at the office and retrieved the camera. The Experiment Station was set back from the road. The grounds were beautifully landscaped and the only modern building, the office, blended well with the old cabin that housed the museum. There was a large outdoor pavilion with a huge fireplace and a long barbecue pit under a low roof supported by stone work columns. The place had been built by the Civilian Conservation Corps during the depression and had that comfortable outdoorsy look to it.

She pulled into the closest parking space available, between a new Chevy sedan and a large four-wheel drive Ford pickup. She tossed the strap of the large tan leather bag over her shoulder and slid out of the car. As she did, she noticed the man approaching the neighboring pickup, her neighbor, the owner of the hounds from hell. Well, now was a good a time to tender the apology she knew he deserved. He looked a lot more civilized now in a tan sports coat and brown slacks. She realized she looked very different than she had out by the garden, too. He stopped between their two vehicles and offered a smile. He really was attractive. Well, Ray had been cute, too, and look where that got her. She approached with a slight smile and her hand outstretched. "Hi, remember me? Your neighbor, Casey, and I want to apologize for my behavior this afternoon. I shouldn't have reacted like that. "

He reached for her outstretched hand and a spark of static electricity flew between their fingers. He touched a nearby car. "I guess you and I are opposites, electrically speaking, of course." He took her hand again. This time he held it a moment longer than was necessary for politeness. Casey could have sworn electricity still flowed between them. "No harm done. I'm Lee. I will fix your garden and put a little fence around it for you so the pups can't get at it again."

"Thanks. They really are just cute puppies."

"I've just had them a few weeks, but I've gotten quite attached to them and probably aren't as firm in disciplining them as I should be." He smiled, showing a dimple and even white teeth. "They are like my kids."

She grinned back. "Yeah, I know how you feel.

I'm like that with Smokey. Well, I guess I had better get in there. I have to cover it for the paper."

"Oh, you're the reporter from the Bugle?"

"Yep. That's me. I've got to interview the new supervisor, some old foggy professor type that specializes in weeds. Can you believe that, all the problems people have with growing plants and they send us a Kudzu expert?"

His grin was sort of lopsided now. "If you wait till I get my briefcase out of the truck, I'll walk you in."

"Oh, I thought you were leaving."

"No. Just need to retrieve some pamphlets I had out here. I need to give a speech later and wanted these for handouts." He opened the battered briefcase and took out a tri-fold pamphlet to hand her.

As soon as she saw the photo on top, she realized her gaffe. "You're not...?" But she knew he was. She could feel her face turning as red as her favorite tomatoes.

"Yep. Dr. Leopold Schmidt, Lee to my friends."

Casey wished a sinkhole would open up in the parking lot and swallow her. "Oh, my god, what can I say. I'm so sorry. I've insulted you twice in one day. Really, I'm not usually such a catty person. I'm just tired and ..."

"It's ok. No offense taken. Perhaps, I'll explain the importance of Kudzu in our interview at Bodine's when we can escape here." He took her arm and began steering them in the direction of the pavilion.

"Bodine's? I thought everything was going to be here," she asked, more confused than ever.

"It is, but as soon as this is over I'm going to Bodine's to get a decent dessert and coffee to top off their truly horrible sandwiches you get at receptions for 'old foggy professors'."

She blushed again. "I'm afraid you'll never let me live that remark down."

"I will, but only if you let me explain the importance of Kudzu over dessert at Bodine's."

"Okay. We'll do the interview at Bodine's." They separated at the pavilion as he went towards the makeshift podium and Casey drifted over to say hello to Velma Lou, who was staring attentively at a tall thin man with a dark moustache. Dirk Campbell was the mayor and, if rumor was to be believed, Velma Lou's latest conquest.

Velma Lou extracted herself from her companion. "Excuse me, I have to give my reporter some last minute instructions." She pulled Casey towards an unoccupied table. "Who was that hunk you came in with? I sure have never seen that kind of beefcake around here before."

It was Casey's turn to smirk. "That's the 'old foggy professor'. Dr. Schmidt."

"Wow! If I knew he was going to be a dead ringer for Mel Gibson, I'd have done the interview myself."

"His looks have nothing to do with it for me. This is strictly business," Casey responded.

"Just because you're coming out of a bad marriage shouldn't cloud your objectivity if you want to be a good reporter and, objectively speaking, he's gorgeous."

"Well, I'll just do my job and interview him, then I don't care if I ever see him again or not. I guess I will see him though since he's my closest neighbor. He just moved into the Stuart House."

"Really?" Velma Lou perked up even more. "That house used to belong to some of my distant ancestors. I went all through it when it first went up for sale. It will take a lot of work to make it livable. He's not going to tear it down, is he?"

"I don't think. Why?"

"Oh, if he does, I might like to buy some of the old trim work. It has some sentimental value to me."

Casey shrugged and moved away toward the front of the room. She couldn't picture her practical cousin as being sentimental. And the modern brick house Velma Lou lived in would not lend itself to trim taken from a nineteenth century Federal style house.

Lee arranged his notes on the podium. Dirk Campbell had moved over to the podium to greet him. Lee had noticed him speaking with the voluptuous looking blond Casey had approached. "I see you met Velma Lou's newest henchman."

"Velma Lou?" Lee asked.

"That's right. You haven't met our local editor." He jerked a thumb in the direction of the two women. "Velma Lou looks like a real southern belle in that low cut red getup but don't let the packaging fool you. She's a cross between Dolly Parton and a shark. That new reporter is quite an eyeful, too."

Mayor Campbell obviously had an eye for the ladies, Lee noted. "Casey turned out to be my neighbor. She lives in that little log cabin down the hill. I'm giving her an interview about the value of Kudzu after the reception."

Campbell continued to stare at the two women. "If I got her alone, I wouldn't want to talk about Kudzu," he commented.

After he had done his duty with the speech and met all the town dignitaries and a good percentage of its citizens, Lee had enough. He spotted Casey's red curls through the crowd and headed her way. "Let's cut out. I'm in the mood for some pecan pie and a real cup of coffee."

He insisted on taking his truck, and agreed to bring her back to get her car since the station was on the way back home from the restaurant, which was, located downtown on the town square. They exchanged small talk about the reception until they reached Bodine's. The place was designed like a small French café. It had a patio in back, with candle lit tables and tiny white lights strung through the trees. Their food was the best in town and the desserts could hold their own with any place in North Georgia. Lee steered them to an outside table. "It's too pretty a night to be inside," he stated. At night the lights twinkled on the mountainsides, making it almost as beautiful a scene as the daytime view of smoky mountains fading from green to purple as they merged with the clouds in the distance.

Lee went with his usual pecan pie and coffee. Casey opted for the Chocolate Decadence, a concoction composed of a brownie covered with vanilla ice cream coated with chocolate topping, then drenched in fresh raspberries and covered with whipped cream, and a cup of Earl Grey Tea.

Instead of the usual cut and dried interview, Lee found himself telling her the story of his life. Growing up in Atlanta, discovering the mountains in his teens and loving them. When he graduated from the University of North Georgia in Athens with a degree in Agricultural Science, he stayed in school to work on his masters, and finally a doctorate. Kudzu, the terror of Georgia farmers, was a subject that interested him. If there were any good uses for a plant that locals claimed you propagated by tossing a cutting on the ground and running before it engulfed you, it would be invaluable to farmers throughout the south. "After all," he explained, "Kudzu is like the South. You can't stomp it out. It's here to stay, so why not enjoy it?"

"Do you mean the South or the plant?" she queried.

"Both." He chuckled. "After all, Kudzu has been in this country since 1876. It might never be considered a 'Native Son', but it's now part of the Southern culture as well as the scenery. It was first introduced at the Japanese Pavilion of the Centennial Exposition in Philadelphia. In Japan, it had long been used as a source of fodder for cattle as well as food for humans. It's related to our common Black Eye Pea, so no wonder it adapted so well in the South."

"To be honest," she admitted, "I never gave it much thought. It was always part of the landscape. I just thought it belonged here."

He explained that the plant had originally been thought to be the salvation of the cotton farmers in the south because of its nitrogen fixing ability and its rapid growth. It would prevent soil erosion, provide an inexpensive fodder for cattle, and send the sagging depression era economy of the South skyrocketing. When farmers realized that their "savior" was in control and refused to be eradicated, it was considered a pest. Millions in government and private money were plowed into the eradication efforts to no avail. Kudzu was here to stay. "So," he concluded, " I began to look for the silver lining. Kudzu has a lot of traditional uses in Japan. Here, there are some people working on it as a cure for alcoholism. A professor at Tuskeegee University has successfully introduced Angora Goats as a solution to part of the problem. The goats thrive on Kudzu and they graze it down enough to prevent unwanted spread. The wool provides a new product for the farmer. For the small farmer, Kudzu is a manageable crop. There is good progress in making paper and cloth. It also provides crafters with a unique vine for basket weaving."

He skimmed over a lot of his personal background. He didn't tell Casey the reason he continued pursuing first his masters, then his doctorate, was due to one small fact. Carole, the woman he dated, announced she was pregnant. Carole was pursuing her master's degree in social sciences and wouldn't hear of moving to the isolated mountain area. They were married and he was able to work as an assistant, and finally an associate, professor, as he continued towards the coveted Ph.D. Carole had a miscarriage and lost the baby, but he felt he owed it to her to try and make the marriage work. Both of them were offered contracts to teach at the college and life was predicable, if not exciting. He had almost given up his dream of the mountains. That is, until his marriage fell apart. It happened midterm last year, when he came home early and caught Carole and one of her students in bed together. They got a civilized divorce and Lee revived his dream of the mountains. He put in for and was accepted as supervisor, largely due to his expertise on Kudzu.

When they got ready to leave the restaurant, Casey reached for the check. Lee covered her hand with his. Both were surprised at the tiny jolt of electricity that coursed through them. "No, Casey, I insist. I have really enjoyed the evening."

"Un un, it's a business expense. I've got it," she asserted.

"Maybe next time. This one's mine." He pulled the check from her grasp and signaled the waitress.

They drove back to station parking lot in companionable silence. Lee realized he knew almost nothing about his companion. Why should he care, he shrugged mentally, he had no intention of ever letting any woman get her hooks in him the way Carole had. Still, he couldn't discount the electricity that tingled up his arm whenever he touched this woman.

Casey drove slowly and carefully around the mountain road. She tried not to hit her brakes and remembered to put her car in low gear so it would climb and descend the curves better. She couldn't keep her mind on the driving, however. She kept remembering the way it felt when Lee had touched her hand. She didn't like the way this man's touch had caused sparks to shoot through her body. She had no intention of letting any man treat her like Ray had.

As Casey pulled up to her cabin, the hair on the back of her neck stood up. She noticed the front porch light was on. She was sure she had not turned it on when she left. It did allow her to see where she was going as she ascended the steps. She reminded herself to turn it on when she would be out after dark. She remembered how Granny Weesie had always left the light on when they were out after dark, and decided she must have subconsciously turned it on without realizing it. She took out her key and inserted it in the lock, then realized it was not locked. She was positive she had locked the door. People in the mountains never did but she had been living in the big city too long to be comfortable with that habit. Even scarier, the rocker was rocking as if someone had just gotten out of it. Since Smokey was lounging on the small table next to the rocker, she assumed he must have just moved from the chair, causing it to move. Anyway if anyone had been here, he would have run like the wind. For an eighteen-pound tomcat, he was a terrible chicken. Since he had his own cat door, he could have disappeared into the cabin at the first approach of any stranger. She carefully pushed open the door and switched the living room light on. Smokey ran in ahead of her and headed for his food dish. Nothing appeared disturbed. She checked the kitchen, bedroom, bath and tiny office, then proceeded cautiously up the steps to the loft. No sign of anyone in any of the rooms. The one tiny closet was jammed with her clothes and miscellaneous items she couldn't find room for in the tiny cabin. She was probably just getting absent minded and forgetting what she was doing. With all the strain she had been under during the divorce, it was surprising she had a mind left.

Even after a soothing bubble bath, Casey was too keyed up for sleep. She started at every night sound. She wasn't used to the wood's noises yet. She still expected to hear traffic and voices, not whip-o-wills and hoot owls outside her window. The closest thing to city lights was the gleam emanating from the house up the hill, Lee's house. She shook off the thought of him settling his long lean frame into his bed. She had been planning to rearrange the furniture to make more room in the small bedroom. Now was as good a time as any.

It was after eleven when she finished moving the last piece. The old oak bed now sat up against the wall next to the window. She remembered rubbing the sturdy round globes on each post when she was a toddler and this was granny's room. The matching waterfall vanity, dresser and chest of drawers looked better in their new spots. She just needed to put the little round table next to the bed.

She decided, much as she loved it, Granny's old woven oval rug was too disreputable to save. Perhaps she would buy one of those hooked ones made by the woman who had a stall at the weekend flea market. Crowds would gather around her tiny stall and watch her work on the rugs. She had told Casey she learned to make them from her mother when she was just a small child, and now selling them to the tourists was her only way to supplement the inadequate social security check she received. Each one was a different work of art. The woman told Casey that when she was a child, the rugs were made from homespun but now she had to use old clothing since nobody wove anymore. She proudly stated that she still made her "own dyes from bark and roots. "Burned up a coupla' ol' iron pots in my time cooking the dyes but you cain't hardly git the ol' colors from commercial dyes."

Casey rolled the rug up and decided to sweep and mop the ancient oak puncheon floor before she turned in. The name had fascinated her as a child, so it had stuck in her head. When she was older, she had looked it up and learned that it just meant the floors had been made from logs that had been cut flat on one side. The ones in this cabin had been cut on both sides making rough planks of about three inches thickness. The years had worn them to a soft smooth finish that Casey loved. She would never trade them for wall-to-wall carpet or tile. As she stepped in front of the little table, she felt one of the boards give a bit. The bed had covered it before so she hadn't noticed it. Now it was decidedly loose. Even though it was just one short plank, it would have to be fixed before it became a hazard. She pushed down with her hand and the board popped up at the other end. There appeared to be something underneath. She raised the board a little more and discovered a black book nestled there. It was dusty and decrepit looking, but had to have been put there by Granny Weesie many years ago. Reverently, she pulled it out and replaced the board.

She opened the front cover. Inside in a childish scrawl were the words "Diary of Louisa Anne Garrett, 1879". My god! This was Granny Weesie's diary when she was just a little girl. Casey cradled the precious book to her heart. It was like a message from Granny when she most needed the comfort only the old woman had ever offered Casey. She turned out the overhead light and switched on the bedside lamp. She lay down on top of the patchwork quilt her great grandmother had made long before she was born and began to read. Smokey curled up at her side.

*T*he funeral were held today. It was in the gloming stead of morning time. An I guess that's fittin seein as how he died. But he were a good man no matter what. He were a beautiful man, too. Folks don't think about how good he was to all us mountain people. They jus talk about how he died. Out there in that barn. Waiting to meet with some woman while Miz Carley were to home tending their young un. Theys all wonderin who it was he was seein an ifn it were her that kilt her lover or ifn she had a jealous man what did it. No un blames Miz Carley. She is always right sickly and could na done it even ifn she caught Reverent Jonathan with a another woman. They is all wonderin. But I know! Yes, an how I wish I never went to that barn night befor las.

Casey laid the book down for a second to rest her eyes. The old mountain speech patterns were distracting to read. She wondered whose funeral. When she opened her eyes, she was no longer in the old bed. She wasn't even in the cabin anymore. She was standing in an old churchyard with a group of people. They were all gathered in front of a rough pine coffin placed in front of a newly dug grave. She must be asleep and dreaming! She closed here eyes again and prayed that when she opened them she would be back in Granny's bed. She had to be in bed dreaming! Where else could she be? But when she opened her eyes, she was still in the old church cemetery. She tried to scream herself awake but no sound came out of her mouth. She looked down and saw her hands and the front of her dress. She was wearing a gingham skirt that hung to her ankles. Her shoes were the old fashioned black high top buttoned variety worn around the turn of the century. Her hands, no the hands of the person she had suddenly become, were those of a child. She realized that she and all the others present were singing "Amazing Grace". It was the strangest feeling. She was still Casey but it was as if she was hiding in a small corner of Louisa's mind. She could observe and hear everything but she had no control over what Louisa said or did. She knew things that were in Louisa's mind, but Louisa seemed not to be aware of Casey at all. It was as if she were reliving young Louisa's life but had no control over the outcome. She was just along for the ride.

This is not real! This is not happening! It is just a dream! But the dream, or vision, or whatever continued. She found she was aware of some of the thoughts in the mind of the child. She knew she was Louisa, her great grandmother. She, Louisa, was thinking about the dead man who she knew as the local preacher. His name was Jonathan Saunders and he had come from some big city outside the mountains to preach the gospel to these people. She knew she was the youngest child in the family. She was thirteen. The others were two brothers and her oldest sister, Lillith, who was twenty-seven.

She looked around. The church was a fairly new

structure. It was built of rough-hewn boards and painted white. The cemetery was next to it and had a variety of headstones scattered around. There were about thirty or so people gathered for the funeral. The man conducting the service was a young man, Daniel Murcott. He was a distant cousin of Jonathan's and had been visiting the preacher's family. He was about seventeen or so and planned on becoming a preacher too. He had a marked resemblance to the dead man. If she squinted a bit, it was almost as if Preacher Jonathan stood there.

Her father, Rob Garrett, stood beside her. He was wizened and appeared to be in his late sixties. He wore a shabby black frock coat that hung on his gaunt frame. Only touches of red remained among his gray hair. Her mother, Hattie, also looked gray and gaunt. Even her sparkling green eyes were glazed with age and hard living. She could have been anywhere from fifty to sixty, but she knew her mother's age was really forty-three and her father was forty-six. The widow, Miz Carley, was the only one seated. She clearly was not healthy and the shock of losing her husband in such a terrible way was too much for her. She hugged a little boy of about two or three who squirmed in her lap.

Her "mother" nudged her as she glanced around. "Stop fidgeting, chil' an' pray for the preacher's soul."

"Yes, Ma," she replied.

After the last hymn, everyone filed past the coffin to say a last good bye to Reverend Jonathan. The coffin was made of a plain unfinished pine. Inside, it was lined with a coarse black cotton cloth. Miz Carley and the child were the last to go to the coffin. The preacher's wife just brushed her lips on the dead man's cheek. The baby tried to hug his father, but his mother turned and walked away from the rustic coffin and the earthly remains of her faithless husband. The woman's eyes flickered briefly over the Garrett family and stayed for a moment on Lillith, the older sister. To Louisa/Casey, it appeared everyone in the churchyard followed that look and allowed the unspoken question that must have been in all their minds to be almost vocalized; what was Lillith Garrett's role in the preacher's death?

Even though she was only thirteen, Louisa knew she would never love another man like she had loved this man. The tears would not be held back. When the service was over, they all gathered around the long rough-hewn picnic table and benches under a little shelter in the churchyard. Lots of food had been set up there. She knew all the womenfolk had made a special dish for the gathering after the service. She had helped Ma make a big iron spider full of baked grits and pork. The grits had been ground just right on the new stone mill Mr. Shook had set up last fall. They had used some of the cheese Ma had made last month. The hens had been especially productive, so there were lots of eggs in it. Thinking about it made her hungry. She hoped Miz MacDougal had made her usual Black Walnut cake. Those walnuts were so good, but so hard to hull. It always tasted better if someone else had done the hard work. Louisa got a heavy crockery plate and stood in line to get her share of the food.

The men all sat around one table and waited for the women to fix a plate and bring it to them. Her sister, Lillith, fixed two plates and went over to a place near the end of the table where only one man sat alone. Louisa noticed she had unbuttoned the top two buttons on the dark red dress she wore. Da would switch her legs if he saw but she had her back to the rest of the group. Several of the old matrons were watching her with cold eyes.

She leaned over to place the plate in front of Donald Stuart and Louisa knew he was staring into her dress right at her bosom. Lillith was enjoying what she was doing. She tossed her long golden curls in the direction of the woods behind the church as if she was inviting him for a walk in the woods. Her deep blue eyes were flashing beneath the long curling lashes. Louisa knew when Lillith got him there, she would do a lot more than just show him her bosom. He shook his head and Lillith flounced away. She dished up another plate and, with a quick glance at Donald, she marched over to his brother, David. The two of them sat for a few minutes, then Lillith slipped off in the direction of the woods. David cast one victorious glance at his brother and followed.

Her sister had a beautiful body and face, but she had no shame. But then, who would expect shame from an adulterer who had murdered her last lover. Louisa knew she should tell the sheriff what she had seen. She also knew her sister's secret was safe. In the mountains, family is important. Blood is thicker than water.

W hen Casey awoke, the sun was streaming in the cabin window. She looked down and found herself clad in the old tee she was wearing when she lay down to read the diary. She was Casey again. The old book lay innocently by her side and Smokey was meowing for some food. It had to have been just a strange dream. But she couldn't forget looking down into that coffin at the handsome preacher - and seeing the face of her neighbor, Lee.

The "dream", coupled with the mysterious occurrences last night, had her rather disoriented. Luckily, it was Sunday and she didn't have to report in to the office. First things first; she put down some cat food for Smokey. He thanked her by rubbing around her legs, nearly tripping her before he dug into the fresh food. Since it was later than usual, she decided to make a festive brunch instead of breakfast. It only took a few minutes to put together some scones, one of Granny Weesie's favorite old recipes. While they were baking, she fixed a cup of tea and decided to eat on the back porch.

Casey brought out a jar of lemon curd and some raspberry jam. A noise in the direction of the garden drew her attention. What an eyeful! Lee was hard at work digging postholes to enclose her garden. He was wearing only a pair of tight Levi's that displayed the contours of his tight rear to advantage. His shirt had been tossed on the grass and his broad shoulders and tightly muscled back were glistening with a light sheen of sweat. If she had been in the market for a new man, he would have been enticing. She sternly reminded herself she was definitely not going to get interested in any man. But at least, he was one who kept his promises. Besides, she would have to have been dead at least several days not to notice that the man had fabulous buns. Neighborliness required that she invite him up for some scones. "Hey there, Lee," she called. "Come on up."

He looked up towards the porch and waved. He stopped and picked up his shirt and headed up as he shrugged into it. "I was just putting in the posts. I didn't want to wake you by doing any tilling."

"Thanks. Would you care for some scones and tea or coffee?"

"Scones! That sounds great. Tea will be fine." He stood next to the chair and she realized anew how tall he was. Probably six one or two. Much as she tried to avoid noticing, she couldn't help but be aware of just how well his worn Levi's fit. "Can I help with anything?"

"No thanks. I just need to get the tea and the scones are still in the oven. Just sit down." She went inside and filled a small pot shaped like the Cheshire Cat with boiling water and put in two tea bags. The sugar and cream was already out there. She put another cup, several saucers and silverware on a tray and added a few apples and some grapes. She had planned to use a paper plate but with company the real thing was more festive. She told herself she would have done the same for a girl friend. The scones were ready by this time so she pulled them out of the oven and put them in a napkin-lined basket.

Lee was impressed. "I've been eating frozen pizzas and TV dinners for several weeks now. Real food sure looks good."

"Don't you cook?"

"Actually, I love to but I've been renovating the house and I just haven't had time. Besides, the kitchen is all torn out. I am just getting it back together. When I do, I'll invite you for dinner," he promised.

She found herself telling him about the lights and unlocked door last night. He was concerned about her investigating on her own. "You probably did forget but you can't be too careful. You should walked up the path to get me or better still, you should have driven around to my place."

"My great grandmother lived here alone until she died at 104. She never locked the door," Casey responded. "She left it to me and no one really lived in it for over thirty years. Mother used to come up once or twice a year and 'air it out'. Then when I was older, I came every now and then. No one ever vandalized it." What she didn't say was that she would have come more often, maybe even lived here, but Ray had hated the place. He was always after her to sell it.

"Even here in the mountains, crime is seeping in. I've been visiting here for years, too. I can see a change. New people keep coming here. Some of them aren't as respectful of other people's property as the mountain people."

They chatted a bit but Casey couldn't bring herself to tell him about the experience with the diary. She was sure he would think she was crazy. He admired the old cabin and she led him on a tour of it. It felt odd showing what she still thought as "Granny Weesie's cabin" even though it had been hers since she was five years old. Showing it to someone else like this, she saw it through his eyes. First growth chestnut trees had been cut, squared and notched, then carefully fitted as tightly as possible so as not to leave any more cracks than necessary for the cold mountain winds to sneak through on bleak winter days. The walls had been paneled with poplar as well and it gave the entire place a warm cozy feeling. He admired the craftsmanship of the long dead woodworker who had fashioned the masterpiece of carefully fitted wood walls and the small round window near the old fireplace in the living room, commenting, "It's hard to believe they did all this without electric tools. Just a bunch of folks would get together and work to build a new neighbor's house. By the end of the day, their new neighbor would have his home. Carpenters today would die if they had to attempt such a job." He thought the big old-fashioned kitchen with its white fifties vintage stove, red and white enamel table and red vinyl chairs fit the place. The matching red trimmed white cupboard with its slide out enamel shelf made it look like one of those "G.E. model kitchens you see in a museum". "You have to draw the line between rustic ambience and modern convenience," was his comment when he noted her microwave and new side-by-side refrigerator.

The office with its computer and file cabinets had nothing of the antique about it. She gestured towards the Foxfire Books and several other volumes about mountain folklore on the shelves. "One day, I'm going to write a book," she confided.

She had not made the bed yet and was going to skip that room, but Lee wandered in before she could change directions. She had no choice but to follow. She blushed when she realized he had to be visualizing her in bed when he looked at the tousled covers. Then found herself blushing even more when she couldn't help conjuring up an image of him in bed with her. You're not going down that road, she reminded herself firmly.

He promised her a tour of his house when he finished the remodeling and said he need to get going if he was going to finish putting up her posts, stringing the chicken wire and running the tiller through her garden before it got too hot. "I'll get you some seedlings in about two weeks," he offered, as he backed down the steps.

She stacked the dishes carefully in the sink. The teapot had been one of granny's favorites. Granny had loved anything to do with cats. In fact, Smokey was a descendant of some of her half-wild cats. Casey had been up here one summer for a few days when she felt the need to get away from Ray for a while. This tiny half starved black cat had drifted up out of the woods and made himself at home on the back porch. She fed him and from that day on, he was her constant companion. Ray had laughed at him when she went back home but didn't have the nerve to make her get rid of him. Smokey seemed to know to stay out of his way, so eight years later she still had him. He was a lazy fat ball of black fluff that weighed eighteen pounds but still was afraid of his own shadow.

She went in to dress the bed. The diary sat amidst the rumpled covers. She picked it up cautiously. It was just a book. Nothing magical or mystical. She looked over the beginning. Strange, the rest of the entry described the scene she had "lived". Perhaps she had read that far, then fell asleep and dreamed it.

She realized how little she knew about her family's history. Her father had died young. Mother had been a real "city girl". Besides, her mother had always treated her as if she were an inconvenience. Standing in the way of her love affairs. Perhaps that was why Casey had rushed into marriage at nineteen, to get away from a home she felt unwelcome in. Only during the summers of her early childhood when she had visited her great grandmother at this little cabin did she feel loved and cherished. After Granny died, the times she had come here with her mother, she had still felt an aura of love and warmth. Her mother hadn't felt anything except distaste for the cabin and had Granny left it to her, she would have sold it long ago. But Granny left it to Casey, with a small trust fund to help maintain it until she was old enough to decide what she wanted to do with it. Although Ray had hated it and begged her to sell, it had always been her refuge when things got too bad with him. When he managed to get almost everything they had owned jointly on the basis of Casey's not working outside the home, the cabin was a welcome haven.

She finished smoothing the patchwork quilt over the bed and lay on top. She decided to read a bit more in broad daylight. She was curious now to know more about the preacher. Did Louisa believe her sister had killed him? The emotions she had "felt" as Louisa certainly were not the type of feelings a thirteen year old today would know. She remembered that girls of that time often married as young as twelve or thirteen in the mountains.

The sheriff come today. I knowed he would sooner or later. He talked to Ma and Da for a while quiet like while I was milkin Ol Bessy. Then he called Lillie off by herself. I seed from the way he looked at her. He weren't going to ask her no hard questions. Nex' he got the boys, Robbie and Matt, they each talked a while. Since he seemed to be going by age, I were next.

The big man with the star pinned to his faded plaid shirt was walking towards her. "Howdy, Weesie," he stooped down, trying to look closer to her size. "Would you feel like goin' for a lil' walk over to the barn and talk to me a bit?"

Louisa/Casey knew it wasn't a real question. If she refused, he would insist. Maybe take her down to his office in town to talk. She had known Sheriff MacDonald since she was a baby. He stopped by to talk to Da often. Sometimes on a Saturday night, he came by and joined in the singing and picking that was a sure bet on the Garrett farm.

"Yes, sir," she replied.

They started walking along a path from the cabin

in the direction of the Stuart house. Only now there was a structure in between. Some sort of old barn with little tendrils of Kudzu around it. It was located where an overgrown thicket filled with brambles and Kudzu stood today, halfway up the hill. "We need to know a few more things about the night the preacher died," the sheriff began. "I believe you was out an' about that night." It wasn't a question.

"Yes, sir. Ah couldn't sleep so's ah took a walk. Moon was full so's ah didn't need no light."

"Did you happen to look at your sister's bed, by any chance?"

"No, sir." That was true anyway. She hadn't had to look at Lillith's bed to know it was empty. "Ah just snuck out and down the ladder."

"Any idea what time it were?"

"Roun' about midnight, ah recon."

"Why don' you tell me where you went and what you did," he suggested.

She drew a deep breath. " Lik' ah said, ah couldn't sleep. I went outside and walked around a while, then ah went back an' got back in bed and ah fell asleep." She didn't tell him any of what she had seen on her midnight ramble. She also didn't mention it had been almost dawn when she finally fell into a troubled sleep. "Nex' thing ah knew, Robbie was wakin' me and tellin' me all about how they had found the preacher shot dead in the old barn and ah heard that old bell tolling. It tolled thirty three times an' I knew it weren't a dream. It had really happened."

He looked directly into his eyes when he asked the next question. "You didn' meet your sister when you were walkin'?"

Since he asked like that, she was able to look him right in the eye and answer truthfully, "No sir."

She twisted her hands in the pockets of her ragged

gingham skirt, ready to cross her fingers if he asked the wrong question.

The next question was a safe one. "Did you see anyone else then?"

"No sir, ah didn't." By now they had reached the front of the barn. Louisa could see inside. She knew she couldn't stand any more questions or she would blurt out the wrong answers. The answers that would put Lillie in jail instead of helping her get to the "big city" like she was always wantin' to do. Even though she had loved Preacher Jon, she couldn't get Lillie in trouble. Anyway, nothin' would bring him back no how. "Please, sir, ah don' feel good. Can ah go home now?"

The big man looked down sadly, "Sure, Child, why not?"

As she, Louisa, hiked back to the cabin, Casey noticed that the trees seemed taller and thicker than in the modern times. She realized that was due in part to the presence of tall straight tree that soared around a hundred feet into the air. The diameters were as thick as three or four feet around. She saw the nuts lying on the ground underneath and realized these were chestnut trees that had since become extinct in the mountains. The air seemed clearer, too. Back nearer the cabin, Lillith was filling a bucket of water from the spring about a hundred yards below the house. When she saw Louisa emerge from the woods, she put down the bucket and stretched her back. She watched to see if Louisa was going to offer to carry it. When she didn't volunteer, Lillith called, "Baby, com'on over heah and help me heft this heah bucket o' water. My back is killin' me somethin powerful."

Louisa knew her back wasn't hurting. She just wanted to find out what Louisa had told the sheriff. She went over anyway and picked up the bucket. "I wish you wouldn't call me 'baby'. I'm too old to be cal't 'baby'."

Although the outside of the cabin had changed only minimally, the inside was a shock to Casey. She had always considered Granny's cabin furnishings charmingly old-fashioned but this was stark. The living room contained just an ancient faded maroon horsehair stuffed sofa with a high back and wood feet and trim that rose in a point along the back top. It was covered with a new basket pattern handmade quilt. The two easy chairs sat on the other side of the room and just in front of the fireplace was a weaving loom. Two cots where Robbie and Matt slept had been pushed up against the wall. A spinning wheel was pushed in the corner and along the wall between the chairs was what must have been a disassembled quilting frame. A high stool sat next to the small round window near the fireplace. A few unmatched rustic tables completed the furnishings. On top of one table sat a large much handled bible. The window had no glass or curtains, just a piece of muslin stretched over them. From the outside, she had noticed solid wood shutters that were probably closed in winter. The only wall decorations were a soulful picture of Jesus and a hand carved wood crucifix. The plank floors were covered with what appeared to be the same oval rug she had just moved out of her bedroom. Now it was new and brightly colored.

The kitchen was an even greater shock. The "fifties look" had been replaced by "early pioneer". Along the wall where the sink was in the present day cabin, stood a long rough-hewn plank table. Over huge crockery bowl hung a small mirror with a honing strap next to it. An open straight edged razor lay next to the bowl. Most of the family's pots seemed to be there. The rest were hanging from nails in the wall. All were heavy black cast iron. If fact, the pots were the only familiar items in the kitchen. Many of them now occupied a place in the cabinet under her sink. The only cabinets in the kitchen now were a series of shelves. These contained a few plates and bowls, some of which were hand carved wood, some tins which contained flour and other staples and various other necessities of life in the late 1800's. Another handmade table and six chairs stood in the middle of the room. Several pitchers and buckets were neatly stacked in one corner. String beans, peppers and assorted herbs hung from the ceiling. In fact, the spicy smell of herbs permeated the entire house. A large wooden bin with two compartments, which someone had made by hand, had a crudely carved image of a potato on one side and an onion on the other.

The stove was the greatest shock. Instead of white porcelain, it was a black cast iron monstrosity that obviously consumed the pile of wood stacked in the corner of the room. It stood about five inches off the floor on legs that looked like animal claws. The front had doors of varying sizes. The largest was an oven. On the left was the firebox where the wood was burned. Directly beneath was the ash box and below the oven, where a broiler was usually located, was a soot drawer where the soot from the chimney fell. The cooking surface had six eyes and about two feet up from that were two warming closets.

"Han' me those leather britches," Lillith asked as she deftly filled one of the large pots with the spring water.

Louisa reached up and took down one stack of the dried beans and passed them to her sister. Without being asked, she proceeded to add a piece of wood to the stove's firebox and then remove an onion from the bin and chop it on the long table. That joined the beans and a piece of salted pork in the pot. Lillith then settled back in one of the chairs, patting the seat next to her. "Tell me what the sheriff asked you."

Louisa obediently sat next to her sister. From her vantage point, she could see her reflection in the shaving mirror. A pretty face framed with auburn curls and startling green eyes stared back at her. She relayed the conversation but didn't comment that she knew anything else. She wasn't sure if her sister knew she had been followed to the barn that night. Lillith sat without speaking for a long while. Then she said, "Shor' was a shame Preacher Jon had to get hisself kilt lik' that. I thought a lot of that man. I shor' did."

"You thought he was your ticket out of here. That the only thing you thought about him."

"Ain't nothing wrong with that. There ain't nothing in these mountains fo' me. I'll jus' get old and worn out like Ma. I wan' to have som' fun. Buy som' pretty things. Ain't nothin' pretty here."

"There's lot of pretty things here. There's the white Dogwood flower that looks like a bride in a picture book an' there's all the wild fruit and nuts, the shiny blackberries, the wild strawberries. Then in fall, the leaves on the mountains turn every color like the world's on fire. Even winter's pretty. The white snow on the ground and the towers of ice on the steep cliffs. Even the foxfire, when we're lucky enough to spot some burnin' at night, that's pretty. An' we always got music in the mountains, the creeks and the little waterfalls all babble at once." Louisa stopped, out of breath from naming all her favorite things. How could Lillith say there was nothing pretty here?

Lillith just shook her head. "I mean the kind of pretty you can buy in a fancy store. We all work from sunup to sundown and never git anything but more work for our trouble. Ain't nothin' wrong with me wantin' to find a man that's take me out of heah and buy me some pretty store-bought things. If I go, I'll fin' a way to get him to let you come live with us and then you can git a man that's somethin' more than a dirt poor farmer."

"Lillie, I love it here. I wouldn' be happy anywhere else. 'Sides, there's plenty wrong with trying to get a married man to take you anywhere. Preacher Jon had a wife and young un."

"Hellfire, everyone knowed Miss Carley was going to die. She wouldn't last past the first snow in the mountains. These mountains are mighty hard on a woman in good health. A sickly puny one don't have a chance," Lillith smiled, knowingly, "anyhow, even a preacher man needs a lil' fun with a strong woman once in a wil'"

"Lillie, why don't you settle in with Donald Stuart? He's powerfully fond o' you."

"Child, time was when I thought Donald was goin' to tak' me away from here. I was jus' a bit older than you are now." She shook her head sadly. "It didn't work. He changed after the war. Mayhaps if'n I don't get away from here befor' I'm too old to find anyone who'll take me where ah wanna be, I'll rethink Donald. I'll be thirty in three years. That's old in the mountains."

The sound of water boiling over and hissing on the hot stovetop startled the sisters.

Casey opened her eyes and sat up in shock. She was back in 2003. The shock was too much. Was she having a nervous breakdown? People didn't really travel back in time. People didn't get a chance to see inside their ancestor's minds. This was not real. It couldn't be.

Casey staggered into the kitchen. Doing the dishes and straightening her nice normal kitchen would bring her down to earth if anything would. When she stepped into the kitchen, a new shock hit her. She had not done anything more than put the dishes in the sink. Now they were carefully washed and dried. To add insult to injury, Granny's old cat teapot was carefully put in its accustomed place on top of the cabinet. The kitchen was now immaculate.

Grasping at feeble hopes, she picked up the phone and dialed Lee. "Please don't think I'm crazy, but did you come back in and do my dishes?"

When she received the expected negative answer, she burst into tears and hung up the phone. She threw herself on the couch and began sobbing. She didn't respond to the knocking on her back door several minutes later. She was too upset to respond even when Lee came and perched next to her and began stroking her hair. "If I thought it was so important, I'd have been glad to do the dishes."

She turned to face him. "It's not that. I'm going crazy!"

He laughed. "You're the sanest person I know"

Between sobs, she poured out the story of the dishes being washed when she awoke. She couldn't bring herself to tell him about her sojourn in the nineteenth century courtesy of an old dairy. When she finished, he looked confused. "I've heard of plenty ghosts in the mountains but never one that washed dishes. Maybe you did them before you lay down to read. Maybe you're dreaming about what you read in the diary. You probably have been under a strain lately." He stood and pulled her up besides him. "Come on down and see what I did to your garden."

The rest of the day passed pleasantly enough. After showing her the once again neatly plowed garden, now enclosed with a low wire fence, Lee told her he would put her plants in by the end of next week, He didn't say when the last freeze date was past and she didn't mention the sore subject. Lee took her in to town for a movie and they stopped for a pizza at Nancy's. He tried hard to take her mind off the strange events and she tried to pretend she had forgotten about them.

Nancy took the order herself and smiled in a friendly way at Casey. She looked a few years older than Casey and had a "local" look about her. "You new in town?" she asked.

"Yes, I've just been here a few weeks. I'd been meaning to stop in and try your pizza for a while now. I'm Katlin Carlson but all my friends call me Casey."

Nancy's smile was a hundred watt one. "Well, I hope you'll stop in often now. You don't need to get anything. Just stop for a chat. You probably don't know many people in town and this is a great place to meet them. Everybody comes in for my food sooner or later. Of course when you have the only pizza parlor in town, that helps."

"I'll take you up on that." Casey liked the smile and felt that this woman could become a friend. She knew she could use one. During the years she was married to Ray, all of her friends had drifted away, repelled by Ray's abrasive personality. Of course, all their joint friends were really Ray's friends.

That night as she prepared for bed, she didn't open the diary. She carefully put it in the bottom drawer of the night table.

When she awoke on Monday, Casey tried to put yesterday's events behind her. *I've just been under too much pressure lately.* She arrived at the office a few minutes late, but still before Velma Lou, and was busy putting her desk in order and chatting with Beverly, the long time Bugle secretary, when her boss arrived. As usual, her cousin's dramatic beauty caused Casey a moment's envy. Velma Lou took one look at the dark circles under Casey's' eyes and commented, "You sure look like something even a polecat wouldn't drag into his hole. Too much night life with that handsome neighbor of yours?"

Casey considered confiding in her cousin but compromised with, "Oh I just found an old diary of my great grandmother's and started reading it. It brought back too many memories of my childhood."

Velma Lou's carefully arched eyebrows raised slightly. She plunked her shapely bottom on Casey's desk. "Anything interesting in the old diary?" She actually appeared interested.

"Well, it's just family stuff. You wouldn't find it interesting. It's just that when I was small, I was so

close to her and the diary brings her so close for me."
What an understatement, but Velma Lou just wasn't
the type of person to confide in. Even if she were,
who in their right mind would tell the boss they were
having hallucinations?

"Remember, I'm family too. In fact, since your
mom's dead and you divorced that louse, Ray, I'm
your only family. Maybe you would lend it to me one
of these days." Velma Lou changed the subject to
work. "I've got a great idea. In fact, maybe your dairy
will help with this. I want you to write a piece for
Confederate Memorial Day. Dig back a bit and find
all the ancestors of residents who were Rebel Soldiers.
Seems I remember my mom saying her Great Uncle
David fought in the war. Or maybe it was his brother,
Donald. He was my great grandmother's father so he
probably wasn't connected with your Great Granny at
all, but who knows? It'll give you an excuse to get
cozy with your new neighbor since they lived in his
house generations back. I hear he's doing a lot of
remodeling. Maybe he will unearth something
interesting." She headed back towards her own office.
" Keep me posted. You should be able to fit in all your
regular assignments with this if you manage your time
well."

Casey looked at the stack of meetings and other
county events she was scheduled to cover and sighed.
Fat chance! This would be a lot more interesting than
the local school board meeting or the county
commission meeting anyway.

By six, she had finished all her copy for the
Tuesday deadline except for the Recreation Board
meeting she was supposed to attend at 8pm. She knew
she needed to grab a quick bite before the meeting if
she was going to concentrate at all. A sub from
Nancy's would fit her mood as well as her
pocketbook. Before she could get out the door, her

phone rang. She considered letting the machine get it but decided maybe it was something important. " Blue Jay Bugle. Katlin Carlson speaking."

"Oh Miz Carlson! Ah'm so glad y're still there! It's Wanda, ya remember me? Ah've got to get outa town quick. Ah need ya help!" The words were all tumbled over one another.

"Yes, Wanda. Of course I remember you. How can I help?" Wanda Folsom was her first story the day she had come to work for the Bugle. Wanda lived out of town in a tangled wooded hollow called Possum Run. Her husband, Zeke, was a real piece of work. He had been abusing Wanda ever since she had the misfortune to marry him at 15. She was now 17 going on 35. This time, Zeke went a bit farther than usual and the police got involved. He beat Wanda so badly that she had to be hospitalized with a fractured jaw and a few cracked ribs. He also started in on their little girl, Rose. Rose had a bruised arm and a black eye. As long as he had confined his violence to Wanda, he could get away with it. She was too frightened of him to press charges. This time was different. The Department of Human Resources stepped in, in the person of Ruby Masters. Ruby was a tiny white-haired woman built like a Greyhound, but when she perceived a child in trouble she was like a Rottweiler. Rose was not going to be abused again if she could help it. She told Wanda in no uncertain terms she had to get her precious child away from "that monster".

When Casey had arrived at the hospital, Wanda was in tears. She couldn't decide if she was more frightened of big brutal Zeke or little ferocious Ruby. Casey soothed the battered wreck of a woman and convinced her Ruby was only trying to help both of them. She had to protect Rose and herself as well. They talked a while about what she would say in court at Zeke's trial and where she would go after.

Ruby had promised to provide help in getting her in the local A.W.A.R. house, a badly overcrowded but safe shelter for abused women. She was also going to try to find training to help her get a decent job.

"Please. Ah need ya help!" Wanda's frightened voice brought her back to the present.

"What do you need, Wanda?"

"Can ya meet me out to the cabin?"

"Oh, Wanda, is it safe for you to go there?"

"Yeah. If you meet me right away. Zeke's still in jail but his brothers are fixin' to get him out on bail in the morning. Please."

"Okay. I'll meet you there in just a few minutes."

She promised her growling stomach a hearty sandwich before the meeting and headed out to Possum Run. The rutted track into the cabin could not be called a road ,any more than the shack with its sagging foundation and torn screen door could be called a home. The black walnut trees hung close to the ground all around and the hollyberry and other close growing scrubs made a wall behind the building. Daylight was fading fast. She wanted to speak to Wanda and get away from here fast. "Wanda, where are you?" she called.

"Ah'm here." A shadow emerged from the porch and came into sight. She was a mess. Her arm was in a cast and a bulky wrapping showed through the thin material of her dress. Her faded blue eyes looked out from a face distorted by swelling and marked with colors ranging from black to yellowing purple. "Ah'm so glad you came. Ah'm goin'a run. I jus' cain't face him in court. Ah'm too afraid."

"Wanda, if you don't testify, he'll get away with this…"

"Ah know. That's why Ah called ya. Ah'm goin'a tell you somethin' that'll put him in jail for a while. Com'on." She turned and led the way down a steep, twisted mountain path.

Casey followed reluctantly. After a few hundred yards, Wanda stopped and began frantically pushing aside some thick blackberry brambles and other tangled vines. What had appeared to be a solid mountainside revealed an opening just large enough for one person to squeeze through. Wanda disappeared into the opening and Casey had no choice but to follow.

Wanda flicked on the small flashlight Casey hadn't even noticed earlier. The cave was barely illuminated but it was enough for Casey to discern the copper kettle set atop a small propane tank and the coils of copper piping. The sickly sweet small of corn mash completed the picture for her. She bolted out the entrance and up the path to the clearing and the safety of her car. Wanda followed.

"Ya see what am tellin' ya. He makes 'shine. Ah can run and ya can show this to the sheriff and he'll still get put away. It's all Ah can do. Don't ya see?" Wanda pleaded for understanding.

Casey understood. "I'll tell the sheriff first thing in the morning. Will that give you enough time to get Rose and go where ever it is you're going?"

"Yes, ma'am. Ah recon' its best if'n you don't know where I'm goin'. Thank you so much." She headed for the rusty 59-ford pickup parked in the shadows. It was only then that Casey noticed a small face peering out of the front window.

"Good luck," Casey murmured under her breath. There were too many "Wanda's" and "Rose's" in this world. She wished she could do more to help. She took the turns and twists in the narrow drive at a much higher speed than felt safe, but she couldn't make herself slow down until she was safely on the main highway and headed for Nancy's. Only one vehicle passed her as she approached town, another rusty ford pickup that could have been a twin to the one Wanda drove except for the scraps of red paint on it. Wanda's had showed just a hint of blue. Ray was bad but compared to Zeke Folsom, he was a prince. She couldn't help thinking what would have happened to her and Wanda if Zeke had gotten out of jail and found them staring at his still.

Business looked slow at Nancy's. Nancy sat at a back table with an ancient looking woman. She was shuffling cards. The door "dinged" when she entered and both women looked up. Nancy motioned her back and dropped the card deck in her apron pocket. "Join us."

"I just wanted a quick sandwich but I don't want to interrupt your game." She slid into the nearest chair, Wanda deliberately relegated to the back of her mind.

The two women laughed in chorus. "It's okay. This is a restaurant. You're not interrupting. By the way, this is my Grandmother, Margaret MacDougal. We were just discussing you." The friendly smile assured Casey the discussion wasn't malicious. "What would you like? I'll go fix it and you can get acquainted with my granny."

"Just an Italian Sub and a Coke will be fine," Casey replied. She turned to the older woman as Nancy headed for the kitchen. It's so nice to meet you, Mrs. MacDougal. I guess Nancy told you everyone calls me Casey."

"Yes. An' please, I'm jus' Miz Maggie. Ain't no un called me 'Mrs. MacDougal' since Teddy was president. You ain't from roun' heah," the bright blue eyes appraised Casey shrewdly, "but you do belong to the mountains." It was a statement not a question.

"My great grandparents where from here," Casey began.

"That's it! I knowed you looked familiar! You're

Louisa Murcott's kin. You have the same look about you she had."

"Why, yes. Granny Weesie was my Great Grandmother. I stayed here with her often when I was a toddler. She died when I was five but I still remember her wonderful stories. I live in her cabin now. My grandmother, Louisa's daughter, died before I was born so Granny Weesie was the only 'grandmother' I remember."

"I knowed you belonged to the mountains! Jus' had that look about you." The old lady beamed.

"Well, my cousin, Velma Lou Dyer, has lived here all her life. I work for her at the paper," Casey explained.

"Pash!" The blue eyes seemed to turn inward. "That cousin of your'n don't belong nowhere.
There's some born here that don't belong and there's some who come here from elsewhere that do belong. You belong to the mountains," Miz Maggie pronounced.

"I gather you knew Granny Weesie?" Casey leaned forward.

"Knowed her well. That sweet ol' woman delivered Nancy's ma."

"I never knew she was a midwife," Casey exclaimed.

"She give it up jus' after Nancy's ma. Said she was gittin' too ol' to be traipsing in the woods all night. I bet there's lots you never knew about your Granny." The old lady looked speculative. "Did you know you look just like her when she was younger? Course she was a good bit older than you when I remember settin' on her porch listening to her tales when I was a young'un. But she kept her looks well, Louisa did. She loved young'uns. Pity she only had that one, Claire, your grandmother. That child was well behaved. Not att'al like her cousin, Anne. Anne would be Velma Lou's great grandmother. I recon there's a case of 'blood will tell'. That young woman was wild as a weed. Course that's what you'd expect, considerin' the upbringin'. Her pa had one floozy after another in that house raisin' that girl. Tain't no wonder she ended up pregnant with no man in sight to claim it."

Nancy returned with the sandwich and drink. The bun looked homemade and the meats and cheeses overflowed its rims. It tasted as good as it looked. "Thanks, Nancy. This is just what I need."

Nancy smiled fondly at her grandmother. "I guess you're been telling her all your old tales. Hope you don't run her away. I can use every new customer I get."

"Not a chance!" Casey replied. "She knew my great grandmother. I want to hear all she can tell me. Besides, she seems to be a fount of knowledge about my extended family."

"I'm sure she can fill your ears for a long time. Story telling is an art form around here."

They engaged in chitchat about local events until Casey had finished her sandwich. She settled her small bill and left. She knew she would return often. Nancy seemed to be the kind of genuine person she needed for a friend and Miz Maggie was a living link to her beloved Granny Weesie. She felt the same sense of belonging the cabin gave her.

Back home, Casey decided to tackle the diary again. The meeting had been boring and uneventful and had lulled the episode with Wanda into prospective. She would call the sheriff first thing in the morning and report the still. Tonight, she kept remembering Miz Maggie's eyes as she told about Granny. There was so much she didn't know about her beloved ancestor. She picked up the book and pulled the old patchwork quilt from the bed. The old quilt had been lovingly made. It was what was called a "Friendship Quilt." Many of the squares contained embroidered names. She couldn't make out many of them and wouldn't know the long dead people even if she could, but the one at the top that was made of blue and had "Louisa Garrett" embroidered in yellow was very dear to her. She visualized a young Louisa and her friends sitting around the old quilting frame in the Garrett living room patiently stitching and gossiping as they put together this link between them and an unknown future. It made her feel so close to Granny Weesie. She took them into the living room and settled into the big old armchair. If she didn't fall asleep, maybe the book wouldn't work its magic on her.

Casey opened the diary to the next entry. She
noted it was dated April 15, 1878. *Donald
Stuart came by to visit today. No one else is to home
now and I think he picked the time so as he could talk
to me private like.*

She opened the screen to let him in and they sat
on the porch bench, Louisa's feet just touching the
wood planks. Donald adjusted his tall frame to the
seat. He pushed a strand of errant blond hair from his
eyes. "Lillith's not here now,." Louisa informed him.

"I know, Little One. I need to talk to you about
something real important."

"Is it a secret?" She always felt comfortable with
Donald Stuart. She liked him so much better than his
twin, David. In fact, of all Lillith's boy friends, she
hoped her big sister would one day settle down with
this one.

"It's a story. And yes, it's a secret too. It started
before you were born. You know I ran away to join
the Confederate army when I was just a young
sprout?"

She nodded. Her green eyes encouraged him to

finish the story.

"In 1864, the war weren't going well. My home life weren't going too well either then. My father was strict. He believed in beatin' David and me for any transgression. David knew how to lie his way out of a lot of scrapes but I wouldn't lie, so I got a lot worse. Ma's health was not good. Lillith was well... Lillith. You know what I mean."

She nodded. She knew exactly what he meant. Lillith had quite a reputation in the area and she had started earning it young.

"So I ran away and joined the army. I guess I reckoned the uniform would make Lillie take me seriously. Even though I didn't like the idea of people ownin' slaves, I loved Georgia. I really believed each state had the right to make its own decisions. Still do. When I came home on leave, Lillie did seem to notice me. In fact she promised to marry me when the war was over, if'n I took her to Atlanta to live. It was a bitter cold February that year, 1865. The whole state was feelin' the devastation of the war we couldn't win. I thought I would need to leave to earn a living anyway so why not Atlanta if it meant so much to Lillie."

He stopped and his light blue eyes took on a faraway look as if he were remembering something both good and bad at the same time. She prodded him to continue. "So what happened? Why didn't you marry her and leave?" His sad eyes rested on Louisa. For a moment she thought he was about to cry. But that was silly; men didn't cry.

"I returned to the war in March. I was reassigned to the troops guarding the President. Then on April second, President Davis got word Lee couldn't guarantee the safety of Richmond. We were assigned to pack everything of value as fast as we could. We stuffed gold and bills into a big black chest and fled just steps ahead of the bluecoats. The chest followed just behind us on the last train out of Richmond before it fell. Mrs. Davis was in tears as she hugged her husband for what might be the last time. Their little girl was holding tight to her daddy's hand as we got on the train. We all knew then that the South we knew was crumbling around us. I think that is the moment when I became a man instead of a little boy pretending he was a soldier to impress his girl. For the next thirty-five days, we played a deadly game of tag with the federal troops. Then on May 5th, the President called his last cabinet meeting in the small town of Washington, Georgia. In the old Georgia State Bank Building, he signed the declaration forever dissolving the Confederacy. I never saw a man looking more bent and aged before his time. I was the only one left guarding the chest that night. Everybody else had fled in panic when they heard the Yanks were coming. I couldn't drag the big chest, so I took the gold out and wrapped it in my coat. I ran for the only place I felt the Yanks wouldn't follow, the mountains. When I got near home, I buried the treasure so it would be safe when the Confederacy organized itself again. But I guess I knew in my heart that it was over. The South was doomed. It was facing a hell even I couldn't imagine." He stopped again and bowed his head.

Louisa probed impatiently. "What happened to the treasure? Where is now? Are you rich?"

"No, my dear child, I'm not rich. In fact that treasure has owned me ever since that fateful night. It wasn't rightfully mine. It belonged to the people of the South. It was made up of the wedding rings of young widows, the heirloom candlesticks of grieving mothers, the watch fobs of no longer rich fathers as they stood at the graves of their young sons who had given much more than gold to the cause. I had to stay and parcel it out to the widows and orphans who had been devastated by the war and its aftermath. Mountain people were poor before but afterwards it was so much worse."

His eyes were envisioning a time before she was born and she was impatient to move into the present with his story. "What did you do?" she breathed.

"The only thing I could do. I stayed here. I tried to explain to Lillith but she wouldn't listen. My father had died just months before. I built a nicer house for Ma with plenty of room for David and me and a wife and children, too." His eyes focused on Louisa for a moment before he continued. "If only Lillie would have understood! As it is, David and I just rattle around like two stones in a creek. We rub each other raw sometimes but he's the only kin I've got."

"So, is the treasure all gone now? Does Lillith know about it?" she asked.

"No, there is a lot left. And yes, I made the mistake of trying to explain to Lillith a long time ago about it. I wish I hadn't told her." He looked thoughtfully at Louisa. "I don't feel so safe since Reverend Jonathan died. I want to move the treasure to the last place they would ever look. After I move it, I am going to give you a letter telling you where it is but don't open it until after my death. Promise."

"Oh, Donald, you ain't gonna die for a long time!"

"One never knows, Little One."

She decided she could trust this man with any secret and the one she carried with her cried out for a confidant. "Donald can I tell you something really bad?"

"Of course, you can tell me anything, don't you know that? I'm your...friend."

"It's about Lillith..."

"Most 'bad secrets' around here usually are." He

chuckled in a way that wasn't really funny.

"The night Reverend Jonathan died…. Well, I followed Lillith. She was meetin' him in the barn." The tears could not be held back. "She went in and then he was dead! I think… I know she …"

"No, Little One," he gently brushed away her tears. "Don't think that your sister did that. I know she was meeting the Preacher but she didn't kill him."

"How do you know," she sobbed.

"Because, like you, I followed someone to the barn. Trust me. Someone else killed him just before Lillie got there." The tight set of his mouth told her the subject was closed. "Now dry your eyes before anyone comes home and finds you in tears. Your family will think I said something to make you cry. Everyone knows you have the sunniest disposition around these parts."

He left her sitting on the porch considering all he had told her. Her mind kept coming back to the fact that he had a real good reason to want the Preacher dead, but she couldn't picture Donald killing anyone. Still he had been in the war and must have killed men then?

C asey awoke with a start. The experience had been more than a dream. Could there really be something to all that mambo jumbo about "spirits" coming back to tell a loved one something? The memory of Granny Weesie holding her on the porch rocker and soothing her to sleep with stories of the "Confederate Treasure" kept coming back, almost as if someone were prompting her to pay attention. Well, whatever was happening, life still continued on a more normal plane. Smokey was meowing to be fed and she had to go to work. She also had to call the sheriff and make a report.

Beverly was working in the back storage room and Velma Lou had not arrived when Casey got to the office, so she figured it was as good a time as any to call Sheriff Cole. He wasn't too happy when she related that Wanda had flown the coop. "Do you realize you're guilty of obstructing justice when you knowingly allow a witness to flee and don't report it?" he growled.

This was not the time for "liberated woman talk". Casey replied in her best Scarlett imitation "But,

Sheriff, Ah am reporting it right now. Your office was closed last night and it wasn't an emergency so Ah couldn't call 911. What do you expect a girl to do?"

"Cut the crap, Ms. Carlson. You're a reporter not a southern belle. You knew you should call me. You just felt sorry for that puny little Wanda and wanted to give her time to escape the clutches of the tough sheriff. Right." It wasn't a question.

"You're right, Sheriff, I'm sorry. Am I going to be in any kind of trouble?"

"Naw. You couldn't have stopped her. Anyway, I feel sorry for her too. Off the record, if she were my sister, I probably would have killed that no account Zeke. He and his worthless brothers give all North Georgians a bad name. Folks see trash like the Folsom's and think all mountain people are worthless hillbillies, wife beaters and moonshiners. Actually this county has one of the lowest crime rates in the country. I just hate to see him walk after what he did to Wanda and that little kid."

"But that's why Wanda called me. I met her out there and she showed me his moonshine still. I can take you right to it."

"I can't get him back in jail where he belongs without Wanda's testimony."

"What about the still?"

"Just your word and the still won't do it. He can claim it isn't his and he had no idea it was there. But I will watch and try to catch him cooking. I'll bring in ATF. You will have to give a statement."

"No problem."

"One more thing. Don't go back out to the Folsom cabin again. If this turns into a story, I'll call you. Zeke is out on bail and he is one mean son of a b-bear."

"Thanks, Sheriff. I want nothing to do with Zeke Folsom."

Before she hung up the phone, Beverly called across the office, "There's someone on line 3 for you. He doesn't sound pleasant."

She punched line 3 and was greeted by a husky masculine voice "Ya meddlin' bitch, where's my wife and young'un?"

Casey knew without a doubt who her caller was. "If this is Mr. Folsom, I have no idea where Wanda and Rose are. Out of your reach, I hope. And I do not appreciate being addressed in such a manner."

"'Missterrr Folsom'! Don't you give me any of ya high faluting talk, girlie. I knowed ya was out to my place las' night. I seed ya car comin' from out my way las' night."

Casey recalled the beat up ford she had passed just after leaving Wanda. She breathed a sigh of relief that they both had left when they did. "I really have nothing more to say to you, Mr. Folsom."

"Ya don't, do ya? Well I've got just one more thing to say to ya. If ya mess in my business one more time, ya dead meat. Got that girlie?"

Casey had not stopped trembling when the door flew open and a burst of laughter followed. Velma Lou entered. She was not alone. She had Lee in tow. He seemed enthralled by her conversation. Velma Lou bounded towards Beverly's desk. "We're heading for the chamber luncheon. I'll be back after that." She tossed a look aver her shoulder at her companion who had stopped at Casey's desk. "Unless something interesting comes up," she added.

Lee studied Casey for a moment. "Are you all right?" He ignored Velma Lou who had joined them.

"I'm fine. I just had a disturbing call. Nothing worth delaying your... meeting about," she barked.

Lee seemed to want to linger but Velma Lou was anxious to get going. "Who was it? What did they say that got you so upset?" he insisted.

"It was Zeke Folsom. He is blaming me for Wanda leaving him." Casey felt the tears stinging her eyes. She wasn't sure if they were tears of anger or fear.

Velma Lou didn't give them chance to carry the conversation farther. "Good for Wanda. Zeke is just an old windbag. All bark no bite. He wouldn't have the nerve to attack anyone who could stand up to him." She pulled Lee's arm. "Come on, we're going to be late."

Beverly looked from Casey to Lee, who was reluctantly being ushered through the front door. She went to comfort the younger woman with a sad smile on her face. "It's not serious. Don't worry."

"Oh, Beverly, I know he wouldn't dare hurt me," she sobbed.

"Even with the best intentions. Men usually manage to hurt the one they care about."

"Best intentions? Zeke?" Casey looked at Beverly as if she had lost her mind.

"It's not Zeke that's hurting you," Beverly consoled. Sadly, Casey realized that Beverly was right. But how could she compete against someone as glamorous as Velma Lou? And did she even want to get involved with any man now?

Beverly seemed to know what was passing through Casey's mind. "Forget it. Let's take a coffee break." They settled in the tiny back room where all the odds and ends of running a newspaper seemed to be stored.

"You know, Velma Lou wasn't always such a glamour puss," Beverly confided.

"Really? Have you know her long?" Casey asked more out of politeness than curiosity.

"We grew up here. Went to school together. She was a little on the plump side then but not so bristly if you know what I mean."

"What changed her?" Casey wanted to know.

"A man. What else?" Beverly's laugh was bitter. "Oh, we all were in love with Rick in high school. Richard Logan the third. He was a piece of work. Looked like Elvis when he was first starting out. He dated Velma Lou in senior year. Then they both went off to college in Atlanta. She came home at the end of the first semester sporting a diamond. Telling everyone they were going to get married just before the start of the second term and she was going to get a job and help him get his degree."

"What happened?" Casey asked.

"It seems while Velma Lou was back home during break, Rick had stayed in Atlanta because he had to work at his part time job. Since the dorm was shut down, he stayed with one of his fraternity buddies. Seems the buddy's father was a bank president. To further sweeten the pot, said buddy had a sister. Sara was a plain little thing just getting close enough to thirty to have been called a 'spinster lady' in the old South. She wasn't the brightest candle on the cake either. In fact, she had just one attractive feature, her father's bank."

"Oh, no!" Casey gasped.

"Oh, yes," Beverly confirmed. "Rick and Sara Moneybags got married three weeks after he met her. Velma Lou didn't find out until she went back to Atlanta. She had already told the dean she wouldn't be back. Rick was supposed to have rented them a place off campus by then."

"How awful!"

"It really was. Velma Lou never talked about what had happened. Of course, the whole town knew. Can't keep a secret in a small town. There was even whispers that Velma Lou was pregnant but no one ever knew for sure."

Casey tried picturing her glamorous cousin in

such a heartbreaking situation. She couldn't. "An experience like that is bound to change a person."

"It did. She didn't come back to town for almost a year. When she did, she didn't tell anyone where she had been all that time. Her dad was the only family she had left. He was still running the paper, but he was pretty deep into the bottle by then so nobody really tried to help her. But I don't think she would have let anyone get near her. She was kind of like a wounded animal that wouldn't trust anyone anymore."

"You still get that impression of her now," Casey remarked.

"She changed physically then too. She lost a lot of weight and started experimenting with makeup and hairstyles. When her old man died, she started changing the paper until it was making a profit for the first time. In the beginning, she really drove herself and everyone else to make the paper succeed. I remember asking her one time if she wanted to be the richest woman in town as well as the prettiest. She looked at me with the saddest look I have ever seen and answered, 'I can't spend pretty. Its only use is to get money. That's the only thing that people value.' I never forgot that and every time I see her flirting and teasing a new man, I remember the hurt young woman she was back then."

"I guess I had better get back to work." Casey broke the mood and headed for her desk with a somewhat different feeling about her cousin. Still, why play her games with Lee? He wasn't rich enough for Velma Lou to be seriously interested. The real question was, was she herself "seriously interested" in the handsome scientist?

The rest of the day dragged by. Velma Lou did not return to the office. She did call just before Casey left. Beverly wasn't at her desk, so Casey answered.

"Hi, Casey. Just wanted to check in. I got detained and couldn't make it back. Any news happening?" Casey could hear water running and a man's voice in the background.

"No, nothing interesting happening here. I'll transfer you to Beverly," she hissed and slammed the hold button down. "Our boss on line 2, Beverly. I'm out of here." She was through the door before Beverly picked up the phone.

When she pulled in the steep driveway leading to her cabin, she couldn't help but notice no lights were on at her neighbor's house up the hill. Resolutely, she turned her back and tried to put Lee out of her thoughts. They deserve one another, she tried to tell herself.

Smokey began intertwining between her feet before she reached the steps. He was acting strangely. She stooped to pet him. "I need to get inside so I can feed you. Stop trying to keep me out here."

When she unlocked the door and threw it open, she wished she had obeyed Smokey's silent warning. She looked once towards the silent dark house on the hill, then decided she had to brave it. What she could see from the door showed her that the front room of the cabin had been thoroughly ransacked. Suppose whoever did it was still there? She should leave and go to a phone. She entered anyway, reasoning that if the burglar were still there, he wouldn't have re-locked the front door. She went only as far as the phone in the kitchen and rapidly dialed 911.

Sheriff Cole arrived quickly. Together they assessed the damage. Most of the house, including the loft had been trashed but in the bedroom, only a few items had been thrown around. In the rest of the place, drawers had been emptied, lamps knocked to the floor. Surprisingly little actual damage had been done. Casey could find nothing missing. Even the dairy that she hadn't been able to find in the night table drawer where she was certain she had put it turned up tangled up in the old quilt.   The sheriff stared into the bedroom and scratched his head, "Normally, I'd say that someone was looking for something specific. It looks like when he got in here, someone frightened him away. Maybe the phone rang or your cat made some kind of noise or he was afraid someone was coming. In this case, considering your run in with Zeke Folsom, my money's on him. I'll shake him up a bit but I bet he is going to have a few brothers and some of his no count cronies that will swear he was with them all day."

After trying unsuccessfully to persuade her to stay with a friend for the night, he left with a stern warning to lock the door and put a safety chain or a bolt on first thing tomorrow. After he drove away, Casey noticed how dark the woods looked when there was no one home up the hill. She shivered and decided a good bubble bath in the old ball and claw tub was what she needed.

With just a minimum of straightening up, she curled up in bed with the diary. The nineteenth century might be a safer place for her to spend the night than the present.

The next entry seemed to be several weeks later. The first two words on the page threw her back in time. *Donald's dead!*

She found herself sitting in the loft, sobbing uncontrollably. It was as if she had lost someone close to her. Someone she loved. But she had. The part of her that was now Louisa had loved Donald Stuart like an older brother or a dear friend. He had been found in the woods not too far from here. His rifle lay across his body lengthwise with the butt near his bare feet. One bullet had passed through his skull. The hunters who found the body had summoned the sheriff and he made an almost instant determination of what had happened. Donald had been upset lately. Everyone had seen that. He must have positioned the rifle so he could pull the trigger with his toes and killed himself. He had probably been the one who killed the preacher and the guilt drove him to suicide. Everyone knew he had a motive. The sheriff didn't mention Lillith

Garrett but he might as well have spelled it out since everyone in town knew Donald carried a mighty big torch for her. Everyone also knew she had been slipping around and seeing the preacher.

Louisa was the only one in the village who believed otherwise. Louisa, and the person who had killed Donald and maybe Jonathon. She heard a noise and looked up to see her mother. "Louisa, honey, I brought you some dinner."

"Thanks, Ma, but ah'm not hungry."

"Life goes on, Child." Her mother stretched her weary back. "Life and death are just two sides of the same coin. It's more than the death that bothers you. You feel something else, don't you?"

She nodded.

"Louisa, honey, I suspect you have 'the sight'. It's in your blood. I've always been able to sense things others don't know. I think you have it too."

Again the child nodded.

"It's the Scots blood. Some of us are born with the gift, or curse. I've never known which it is. I think it's worse for me because I have just a touch of the Cherokee blood, too. The violence and the evil, they're just there on the other side of a veil. But they are always there. It's part of this very land we trod upon. You know how we came to have this place. Us and all the white folks?"

"We came when the Indians left," Louisa replied.

"Oh yes, they left. But not because they wanted to. They loved this land. It had been their homeland for generations. We, the white ones, we drove them out on the bloody trail of tears. There are some alive today who remember. We rounded them up and put them in stockades. Then we sent them out to march to Oklahoma and die by the thousands before they got there. We did it so we could steal the gold, and farm the hills, and build our cabins in these woods. The government divided it up by lottery. My grandfather was one who got his parcel, as did all our neighbors. For the most part, they're all good people but the blood of evil soaked this land; perhaps that's why so much evil must happen here. And people like you and me, we see more than most. One of my grandmothers was a Cherokee wise woman. You and I and all our children will always have some of her in us." The older woman laid her hand on the child's head. "There's things I must tell you someday...When you are older. Not yet. You must stop mourning. T'will do no good."

She sat staring out the window for a long time after her mother left. In the distance, the mountains faded from green to indigo to deepest purple as nightfall settled around her little cabin. The sheep had returned home for some reason today. Usually they stayed in the coves, where the grass was all fine bladed and tender, unless you went to hunt them up and herded them home. Maybe they knew it was spring shearing time and came home to give their owners the fine silky wool they provided. They didn't like the tough fescue that grew in our pasture in the spring before Da planted the rye and corn that would feed them in winter. Da gave them a salt lick and they were contentedly sharing the yard with Cain, our mule, and the cow, Ole Bessie, just outside of the little lean to that usually sheltered them in the winter. The lead ram had a bell around his neck that made a kind of music in the soft moonlight. The cicadas made their own brand of music and, when she looked at the edge of the woods where the farm met the tree line, she saw the glimmer of foxfire. When she was a small child, she had believed the flickering lights in the forest were made by fairies and if you followed them you would get lost so deep in the woods you could never find your way home again. Maybe she had followed the foxfire and this was all made believe. Then she realized she wasn't a child anymore.

The next morning, Louisa dressed and came down to have breakfast with her family. She saw that Robbie had gathered the eggs, her usual job. Her brothers and sister gathered around the table. She heard her father's axe outside as he chopped wood. The shrill sound of the axe striking hard wood became a ringing phone and she awoke.

"Hello"

"Girlie, I warned ya to leave me alone! I ain't done ya nothin' yet but ah will. Stay outa my business!" The phone banged down and she was left with the dial tone throbbing in her ear.

Zeke! Yesterday's events came flooding back. Surely he must have known she would call the sheriff.

She staggered out of bed and fixed a cup of mint tea. She spent the next hour straightening up the cabin, then got dressed and drove down to Nancy's to treat herself to breakfast. She wasn't up to cooking today. Lee's truck still wasn't in his driveway. So what, she reminded herself. *I've got no claim on him and that's just the way I want it.* She was in a foul mood when she stormed into Nancy's and slid into a back booth.

Nancy sensed her mood at once. She brought her a cup of coffee with the menu. "Feeling down?" she asked.

"Big time down," Casey replied. "How about one egg, over easy, grits, biscuits and some company?"

"As luck would have it, I have Annie in the kitchen this morning. I think she can manage your order while you tell me all your troubles. I doubt if I can solve any of your problems but sometimes just having a sympathetic listener helps. I can offer you that."

"Great. I do need a friend now," Casey replied.

After the good breakfast, several cups of coffee and Nancy's sympathetic ear, Casey did feel better. She resolved to get to work on the "Confederate Memorial Day" piece in earnest. She would get some gas first, then check in at the office and let Velma Lou know she would be interviewing some of the county's older residents about their grandfathers. Miz Maggie was at the top of her list since Nancy had told her that her great great grandfathers on both sides of the family had been in the war. One of them had been wounded and accorded a hero's status in the town. The gas station she usually used had a long line, so she pulled into a small station just past it. She had just started pumping gas when the mechanic/attendant came up behind her. "Want me to check yer hood?" he asked.

"Why, yes," she replied. She wasn't used to "service" stations. In Atlanta, she had always gassed her own car and checked the usual fluids, only taking it to her trusted mechanic when it was due for an oil change or had some other problem.

He spat a plug of tobacco toward the road and wiped his greasy hands on his equally greasy overalls. He bent over her open hood and pulled the stick. "Oil's okay but you have a real bad spot on your radiator hose that could bust any minute now. Want I should replace it for you?"

She thought of her friendly mechanic in Atlanta. Atlanta was a long ways off in the case of car trouble. "Sure. Thanks for catching it for me." She offered the surly grease monkey her best smile.

He didn't return it. "You need a lift while I'm

doing it?" he asked

The thought of getting in a car with this disreputable unfriendly person was not a pleasant idea. "No, thanks. I'm just going down the street a few blocks. The walk will do me good. Can I pick it up about lunch time?"

"Suit yourself. It'll be ready in about an hour." He turned away, still without the ghost of a smile.

She had only walked about a block when Velma Lou pulled up in her smart little Camara (ck spelling). "Need a lift?"

"Perfect timing." Casey settled into the red leather bucket seat. "I was just heading to the office to start putting the Confederate piece together."

"Any good material?" Velma Lou queried. "Or any other good stories for that matter?"

"Just all the stuff that's been happening to me lately," Casey sighed.

"To you? Has something happened to you?" Velma Lou inquired. "Anything I can do to help?"

She seemed sincere in her concern.

"No." She considered how much of what was happening that she wanted to tell her cousin. "I don't guess there is anything you can do about it." She recounted the last few day's adventures, leaving out her hurt about Velma Lou's apparent conquest of Lee.

"Oh Darlin'," Velma Lou purred, "that's terrible. Of course I can do something about it. I can have you come stay at my place for a while until that terrible Zeke is behind bars for good."

Casey envisioned staying at Velma Lou's and encountering a lovesick Lee as he came to pay court to the gorgeous blond. She shivered with distaste. "No! No thanks."

"Well, I didn't know I was that unpleasant," Velma Lou laughed.

"Oh, no, I didn't mean it that way. It's not you. It's

just…things."

"I understand. Look, I have another idea that might help. I've been thinking about investing in some rental property. Maybe you would want to sell me the cabin…"

"Oh no! I'll never sell the cabin! It was Granny Weesie's. I couldn't."

"Well, it was just a thought. I didn't mean to upset you. I was just trying to help. You are the only kin I have left. You know I really don't want anything to happen to you. Please think about my offer."

"I know. I don't mean to be ungrateful. I really do appreciate your concern." They had reached the office. "Thanks, but don't worry. I'll be fine."

"Okay," Velma Lou replied, heading back to her office. "Just let me know if you need a anything. How about a ride to pick up your car later? When will it be ready?"

"I'll get it around lunchtime. I want to walk; it'll clear the cobwebs out of my brain."

Casey was just getting started on her outline when Dirk Campbell stopped by to see Velma Lou. The mayor stooped at Casey's desk for a minute to chat. He seemed solicitous but there was something about the man that just put her off. It seemed like only minutes had passed when she glanced at the clock and realized it was 12:30.

After picking up her car, she headed towards Miz Maggie's house. According to Nancy's directions, it was near the top of a winding road that led to a spot called "Insurance Peak". The road had earned its name during the depression. Local people who had purchased a car before the depression and found themselves too strapped to pay the notes, often drove them to the top of the ridge and nudged the vehicle over the steep incline. This way, the insurance company would have to pay the rest of the mortgage, letting the owner save face. She realized she was going too fast for such a winding road and pushed the brake. Nothing happened! She pumped it again and mashed it to the floor but nothing happened! A million thoughts and a few prayers flashed through her mind. She considered turning the ignition off, but realized if she did the power steering would go off too and the car would likely careen over the side before she could maneuver it to a stop. The transmission. Yes! She dropped it down into low gear. It helped a bit. If she could only keep it on the road until the next uphill stretch, she would then slow down enough to take a chance on cutting the engine and trying to pull to the shoulder. The car was careening wildly on a steep downhill slope now. Then, finally, an uphill stretch. She clicked the key off. Immediately the car became tank like and sluggish but it worked. She was stopped and on the tiny shoulder adjacent to a steep plunge down a rocky cliff. She stepped out and felt her knees buckle. She leaned on the driver's door and retched. Sweat was pouring off her and she smelled the rank odor of fear.

A decrepit pickup pulled off next to her, "Are you alright, Ma'am?" The driver was elderly and fatherly looking.

"I'm fine now. My brakes gave out. I almost went over," she babbled hysterically.

"Lady, you should always keep your car serviced. These mountains ain't no place to skimp on car repair. I'm going up the road a bit. I can drop you off if you were going to see anyone up here, or I can take you back to town as soon as I make the one stop."

She knew he thought her just a dumb woman who drove her car without ever having it serviced until it left her on the road. She didn't bother trying to tell him the real story. The car had just come from a service station. "Do you know where Miz Maggie lives? Could you drop me off there?"

"Sure thing, Lady. That's right by where I'm going. Hop in."

Maggie fussed over her and fixed her a special blackberry tea to calm her nerves. She called Nancy who promised to be right there. She also gave her the name of a reputable mechanic who could tow the car back to town. After Miz Maggie had assured herself that Casey was all right, she returned to the original purpose of the visit. "While y're waiting, do you want to hear about my grandfathers?"

Casey assured her that she would, and settled back with her tea to enjoy the older woman's story. Miz Maggie's cabin was a throwback to an earlier era. Casey had just glimpsed the living room as she was led back into the large kitchen by the kindhearted old lady. The sofa and chair in the living room was made of local oak branches, curved and shaped to form the back and arms. The seat and backrest were overstuffed cushions covered in a woven material with a beautiful pattern of rose and brown. Hand-knitted afghans were carelessly tossed over both the sofa and chair. The other furniture was of a similar design. A huge fireplace flanked with stonework faced the door.

Here in the kitchen, the other side of the fireplace revealed it as a pass-through that was large enough for a small person to crawl through. Modern architects would have considered it a shameful energy waster. Casey considered it charming. She sat at the long trestle table made from hand-smoothed walnut. Each plank must have been at least thirteen or fourteen inches wide. That kind of stuff didn't grow anywhere now. The chairs of the same wood were softened by small cushions of butternut yellow fabric, as were the curtains at the three windows opening the cabin to a view of breathtaking mountains.

Before beginning her family history, Maggie satisfied Casey's curiosity about the unusual material. "I see you noticed my curtains. I weave the stuff myself from sheep wool. My cousin over in Suches raises sheep. In the days when your granny was a young'un, the sheep was jest tiny things. T'weren't no bigger than a dog. Nowadays, they's much bigger. Ust'r be you got about a pound or two of wool per sheep. Now, my cousin gets about five to six pounds. I card it an spin it myself."

Casey interrupted. "I know about spinning wheels, but what is carding?"

"Here. I'll show you. It's easier than tellin'. Come'n in here." She led Casey into the back room opening off the kitchen. The entire room was filled by a large loom, spinning wheel and various other items used to make cloth. Maggie picked up a pair of tools that looked like huge dog grooming brushes with handles on the sides instead of the ends. "You load the wool on the top one of these breaking cards, then you draw it over the bottom 'un 'til all the wool is moved to the bottom card. You jest swipe it back onto the top card with one swoop. You do that until the wool is in a nice fluffy bat. When you're ready to make it into spinnin' wool, you use these fine cards. See how the teeth are smaller and closer together? You do jest about the same way 'til you get nice rolls. You use the back to roll the rolls firmer, and you get a roll you can spin into a thread."

"That's amazing. All the times I wore wool things and I never thought about what went into making it," Casey marveled.

"That's only the half of it. After I spin the thread on my spinning wheel, " she pointed to the small wooden wheel and pedal device, "then I dye it. I do a warp, then weave it on the loom. See that pattern on my sofa, that's called a 'Rose and Vine'. I got the brown color from Black Walnut hulls. You jest gather a whole mess of hulls and put 'em in a cheesecloth bag so that they won't git all tangled in the skein of wool. You boil them in a big pot and put in the wool skeins. Some folks use a cup of vinegar or salt as a mordant to set the dye, but with the walnut hulls you don't need that. It makes a real pretty brown and won't fade. Now the red I get from pokeberries and that soft yellow is from oak bark."

"They're lovely," Casey exclaimed. "You people up here do so many things in the old ways. It's almost like the past is still alive in the mountains."

"Oh, the past is always still alive." Maggie looked strangely at the younger woman for a moment. "The past ain't always what it's cracked up to be. Well, let's git on with my ancient history so you'll have your newspaper article afore Nancy gits here to take ya'll home."

Maggie knew little of her mother's father except for his name rank and regiment, and the fact that he had returned a bitter man, aged before his time; but her father's father was a different story. The old man had lived to bounce his great grandchildren on his knee. As the story enfolded, Casey was enthralled. This man was a contemporary of her beloved granny. "Charlie Dugan had music in his blood. He went off to war at 17, singing a mountain ballad. He was a natural choice for his company's bugler. Wounded in an act of heroism at Shiloh, he came back minus one leg. Married his childhood sweetheart. Charlie idolized Donald Stuart. Said he wouldna' made it without 'im. Donald all'ays gave 'im money for medicin' and farmin' equipment. Couldna' stand David. Never said why. Jus' wouldna' talk of the man a'tall."

"Perhaps it was because it was because Donald was a fellow soldier?" Casey ventured.

"'Twere more 'an that. I remember David Stuart a bit myself. He were an ol' man when I was just a young'un, but there were all'ays somethin' haunted lookin' about him. Like he'd jus' seed a painter comin' up behin' 'im." The old lady shook her head as if to rid herself of bad memories. "His ol' woman, Lillith, they say weren' no better than she should be neither. No siree. All'us thought that first young'un of her'n was Donald's. Then after she up and died, he kept one strumpet after another in that big house o' his."

Remembering some of her family history, Casey replied, "Miss Maggie, you know that's impossible. She didn't have her first child until November 1880. Donald Stuart died mysteriously in May of 1879."

The old woman looked at her strangely for several seconds. "I keep forgitting you kin to that bunch. I better git to fixin' Nancy some tea. She'll be here 'fore I git the water to boilin'"

Sure enough, Nancy arrived just as Miss Maggie brought her tea to the table. She fussed over Casey and warned her about "riding her brakes in the mountains like a flatlander".

"But I wasn't! I know better than that. I always gear down when I'm climbing or descending a steep stretch of road."

"Well," Nancy replied, "You need that mechanic to check…."

"Oh, my god," Casey interrupted, "I completely forgot to call the mechanic you recommended. I had better do it now."

When she returned from calling to have the mechanic tow her car, she returned to join Maggie and Nancy in the kitchen. "All taken care of. This is getting be a habit."

"What?" Nancy quipped. "Almost driving off the mountain?"

"No, silly, leaving my car in the care of a mechanic. I just had the radiator fixed at that service station just down the road from you. You know, Laz's Place."

The other two women exchanged strange looks. "Did you know that Lazarus is Zeke's cousin?"

"No. No, I didn't. But after meeting him, I can believe…You don't think? I mean he wouldn't do anything… I mean he doesn't know about me or Zeke…."

Nancy nodded slowly. "This isn't Atlanta. News here travels on the wind. He probably knows all about you, and a few things extra Zeke probably told him that aren't remotely related to the truth. And yes, I think. I know, he wouldn't hesitate for a minute to get even with somebody he thought had done his kin wrong. Nobody goes to his shop except some of his no count moonshine swilling buddies."

The two women drove home in silence. At Casey's cabin, Nancy patted her friend's hand. "Joe Taylor is a good mechanic and a friend. He'll be able to tell if anybody fooled with your brakes. Go on now. Try to get some sleep and don't worry. Ya' need a ride in the morning?"

"Thanks, I'm not sure. I'll call Velma Lou and see what's happening in the office. Maybe I can work from home."

Strangely enough, when she ascended the steps of the cabin, she found the porch light on even though when she left, she had paid particular attention to turning it off. She was beginning to accept that someone, something, maybe Granny's spirit, looked after the cabin. This time travel thing was spooky enough without adding ghosts to the new repertoire of her beliefs. She shoved the disturbing thoughts to the back of her mind. Smokey materialized out of the darkness and began twining around her ankles.

"Guess you're hungry, old boy."

She fixed him a bowl of cat food first thing. To do otherwise would be courting a fall, literally, since the big tom circled her ankles until his bowl was set in from of him. He then abandoned her and dug into his dinner as if he had not been fed in a month instead of that very morning before Casey left to begin her ill-fated day.

As she dialed Velma Lou's number, she couldn't help but notice that there were no lights on at the house up the hill. When a giggly voice answered, Casey realized she must have interrupted a romantic interlude at Velma Lou's. Her cousin's voice became more business like as she acknowledged Casey's call. "Jus' a minute', Darlin'. I have to tell a friend good bye."

Off line, Casey could hear what sounded like a long kiss and then Velma Lou's voice. "Bye now, Sugar. I sure did enjoy our evening and everythin'." The emphasis on the "everythin" made it clear to Casey what she had interrupted. The fact that her cousin had left the office with Lee and his lights were still off gave her a pretty good clue who the romantic interlude had been with. Well, so what. Lee was a free man. So was Velma Lou. If he wanted to get entangled with a social climbing slut like her cousin, so what. She could care less. But the more she told herself that, the less she believed it. She was beginning to have feelings for the handsome scientist that were stronger than neighborly. Until now, she had thought he had reciprocated. Well, her experience with Ray should have taught her something about men. Flash a gorgeous and very available blonde in front of them and they stopped thinking with their brain and allotted that function to an organ farther down the body.

She cleared with Velma Lou that it was fine for

her to work from home tomorrow, and heard her cousin's cries of horror as Casey related her day. "Oh, Darlin' why don't you come stay over at my place for a while. Jus' till they pick up Zeke?"

There was no way she would do that, especially now. "How can you be sure it's Zeke's doing?" she asked.

"Well, of course it's him. Who else would want to harm you?"

After completing that phone call, she called the mechanic, not sure if he would still be at the garage. He was, and assured her he had the car there and would start on it first thing in the morning. He would call when it was ready and send one of his mechanics to pick her up. She thanked him and just as she hung up, she noticed a light go on up hill. Perfect timing for a drive from her cousin's house. She wasn't sure he would try to call her but just in case, she left the phone off the hook, turned off the light and retreated to her bedroom. After talking her bath and slipping into a soft old tee shirt, she decided to put the phone back on the hook. All lights were off in the house up the hill and the mechanic had said he would call in the morning. She would snuggle up with Granny's dairy. In her present mood, any time was better than the present.

She opened the book to the next entry. Apparently Louisa hadn't written anything for a while. This entry was dated April 3rd, 1880, almost a year since Donald's death. *Today is supposed to be a special day. My sister is getting married. As I got dressed in my best Sunday go to church dress, I just couldn't feel good about the whole thing. It was just plain wrong. She was marrying the wrong man. Worse, he weren't just wrong for her. He was just plain wrong. He was not a good man like his brother.*

Suddenly she, Louisa/Casey was in her loft bedroom, dressing for the wedding. Her parents, Lillith and her two brothers were out in the yard greeting early arrivals and tuning up their instruments in preparation for the wedding celebration. It was one of those days that seemed to be June instead of early April. The sunlight falling on the blooming dogwood caused the petals to gleam like ivory. The earth gave off a warm feeling as the grasses and spring flowers put on a colorful show. It was one of Louisa's favorite times of year.

She was wearing a brightly patterned dress. It was not new but it was attractive and fit her well. Her parents were likewise dressed in their best. Lillith was wearing a woven dress made of fine white material. The cuffs and collar were dyed an earthy butternut color that set off the wearer's bright golden curls and made her immense blue eyes seem even bluer and bigger. Her sister looked like a happy blushing bride. Just went to show that looks were deceiving. Louisa could not help thinking of the old mountain rhyme that went, "Marry in white, you're sure to fight."

When she stepped into the yard, the new preacher, Daniel Murcott, was the first man she noticed. She had met him when he conducted Jonathan's funeral. She studied him now as he spoke earnestly with their father. The resemblance to Jonathan was strong but he was definitely his own man. She judged him young to have taken on the responsibilities of a mountain church, but he seemed very much in control. His most striking feature was his blazing blue eyes. His strong-planed tanned face was similar but subtly different from his deceased cousin. When those incredibly blue eyes met Louisa's, she felt a lurch in the pit of her stomach and looked away. Was she transferring her strong feelings for Jonathan to this cousin because of the resemblance? Or was it just that she was fourteen and he was a very attractive man.

After the ceremony, they went up hill to David's place. He had a few cousins who were helping him put together the traditional infare wedding feast, usually provided by the groom's family. There were few enough occasions for celebration in the mountains, so even though most of the people around didn't like Lillith, they still turned out. Infare was such a mountain custom that even David, who usually avoided the old traditions, felt compelled to offer the feast and celebration expected from the Appalachian groom. The women all came bearing a layer for the bride's stack cake. Music and dancing would go on until dawn. There was food assembled on the outdoor tables. Lillith flirted and teased her new groom but David seemed preoccupied for a man who had just married the prettiest girl in the area. When his eyes came to rest on the budding figure of his sister-in-law, Louisa shuddered. Something about the way he looked at her made her feel as if someone was peering in her bedroom window while she was dressing. David turned abruptly from his bride and started in her direction. She would have to be polite to the man. He was her brother-in-law now. Family was important. You had to treat them right, but never the less she was glad the new preacher was also approaching her. She smiled at Daniel and ignored the frown on David's face as he turned away and pretended he was going to speak with his new mother-in-law instead.

Daniel looked at her in a strange way, as if he too wanted to see what she had under her clothes, but with him it didn't feel the same. In fact she liked his looking at her that way. She could tell that even though he might be attracted to her, he would never hurt her. She didn't feel that way about David. Ever since Donald's death, she had felt a strange uneasy feeling every time she was forced into David's company.

"Fine afternoon isn't it, Miss Louisa?" he asked.

"It sure is, Preacher Murcott. How are you enjoying your new duties here?" Out of the corner of her eye, she saw David saunter over to his new father-in-law and begin talking as if that had been his original plan.

"It is right challenging. Of course, there is always a need for toilers in the Lord's vineyard. Perhaps the Lord will send me a willing helpmate before long."

Louisa looked across the churchyard to where

David had finally returned to her sister's side. She knew, with a bit of encouragement, the new preacher would start courting her. And why not, she thought. The only man who had made her heart beat faster was Jonathan and he was forever gone. Daniel reminded her somewhat of his cousin. He appeared to be a bit obsessed with "the Lord" but that was much better than forever slurping moonshine out of a jug or running off hunting with the other men like her sister's new husband and so many of the other men around here. Besides, she was all of fourteen and it was high time she started thinking about a home of her own. The preacher had a nice cabin furnished with the church and he was educated, compared to the mountain men. She needed to start watching the way she spoke. She wished now she had paid more attention to the teacher at the little one room school she went to 'til she finished fourth grade. Her parents wanted the best for her but they couldn't afford the forty cents it cost every month to send her to school. Fourth grade was more education than most of the other people her age had anyway. Families needed every hand working to make it through the hard Appalachian winters. There wasn't time for fancy things like schoolin'. She smiled up at the young man who sat patiently at her side. "Mayhaps, you'd care to come to supper at our house next Sunday after church?" She knew her ma would be thrilled to have the new preacher as a guest.

"Why, Miss Louisa, I'd be delighted." He did have a nice smile. It reminded her of Jonathan's.

By the time they returned home, Lillith and David had gone up to their bedroom in the big Stuart house. Both had been nipping at David's jug and as the evening progressed, they seemed more like a pair of tomcats tied in the same sack than newlyweds. David's female cousins were preparing for a shiveree when they left. The banging of pots and pans and the rowdy chants of the folkloric mountain serenade had begun beneath the newlywed's window. She wondered if any of the men had enough courage to give David the traditional ride on a log. Louisa wished her sister well, but she couldn't feel good about anything having to do with David Stuart. He was so unlike his kindly brother.

She made a decision, "Ma, tomorrow, I'd like to visit a spell with Miz Mable about settin' up a quiltin' bee. I reckon I'm ready to start on a quilt for my hope chest. I think I want a friendship one."

Her mother smiled. Everyone knew when a young mountain girl visited the quilt maker, a wedding wasn't far away.

Miz Mable, the local quilt maker, wasted no time. Two weeks later, Louisa and all of the local women were gathered around the finished quilt. Each piece had been painstakingly embroidered with the sewer's name before it was all pieced, then a batting and backing added. "Now," Miz Mable instructed, "fetch one of them barn cats so as we can see who'll be the next un to tie the knot after Weesie and her preacher man."

The young girls all giggled and grabbed a side of the new quilt to hold it taunt while Louisa carefully placed Hoecake, her favorite barn cat, in the middle of the new quilt. The girls all bounced the quilt heartily and Hoecake jumped off. He brushed up against Flora McLeod in his haste to escape this new unsteady perch. The other girls clustered around the fifteen year old and queried about who she was courtin'.

Louisa fingered her new quilt fondly. It would last many a year and warm Daniel and her on cold winter nights.

She awoke the next morning suddenly to what in her dream was shrill birdsong but was actually the phone. She loosened her hold on the old quilt to grab the phone. After assuring Velma Lou that "yes, she was fine" and "no, she hadn't hear from her mechanic" and definitely she didn't want to "leave the cabin to stay at your house until Zeke was arrested", she put on the tea kettle and added some food to Smokey's bowl. The big tom was watching her with sleepy yellow eyes. She had finished her second cup of tea and some cereal and was just getting started on her Confederate Memorial Day piece when the mechanic called. He told her what she had already suspected. Someone had loosened the brake lines under the car so that after driving for a little while, they would come apart and she would have no breaks. "It's highly unusual that both lines would do this on their own at the same time," he concluded.

When she got off the phone, she slipped into some jeans and a tee shirt and awaited the person the mechanic was sending to pick her up. She decided to call Sheriff Cole and let him know what was happening. The sheriff was touchingly concerned for her safety. He agreed to meet her at the mechanic shop and take her report.

The sheriff hadn't arrived when she got to Tom's Engines and Everything Automotive. Tom urged her to "Take'er for a spin and check out how the brakes feel."

She planned to just circle the block but she had no sooner pulled into the street than a rusty red pick-up rammed into her rear. Zeke jumped out the cab and raced toward her. She could see his mouth moving in her side mirror before she could hear him, but she knew what he was saying was not pleasant. Fortunately, before he could reach the front of her car, Sheriff Cole pulled up behind the pick-up. Casey pulled off the road to allow the sheriff to deal with Zeke. Zeke wheeled around and jumped into his pick-up before the sheriff could get out of his car. He sped off, careening wildly around the mountain road. The sheriff jumped back into the cruiser and pursued. Not to be left out, Casey followed behind.

Zeke turned off on a mountain road that wound steadily uphill. She could hear the siren ahead but Casey slowed to a safe crawl. She couldn't forget yesterday's experience. Suddenly, she spotted the two vehicles pulled just off the road near a path. Casey had just found a relatively safe spot to park when another cruiser with two deputies arrived. "Stay outa' the way, Ma'am," they yelled as they raced up the path to assist the sheriff.

Casey decided that "outa' the way" could be interpreted broadly. After all she was a reporter at the scene of a great story as well as an interested party. She strode down the path to a small clearing. Zeke had apparently climbed one of the Black Walnut Trees to a small hunting stand perched in the leafy green foliage. Sheriff Cole, who was a bit on the stocky side, obviously didn't want to try climbing the tree. Neither did he want to shoot a drunk armed only with a handful of black walnuts, which Zeke was lobbing down with surprising accuracy for one whose speech revealed an obviously extreme state of drunkenness.

"Y'ain't goinna tak' me alive, Sheriff. My ol' woman's done gone and lef' me. I cain's hardly cook none. I'd rather be shot by a polecat law officer than stave to death in my own cabin!"

"Zeke, Come on down here, ya hear. You cain't go round attackin' ladies, especially not a reporter lady," the sheriff shouted in the direction the walnuts were coming.

"Dammed reporter lady made my ol' lady leave me. I jus' want Wanda an' my baby back. It's all her fault."

"Naw it ain't, Zeke. Wanda left ya' 'cause ya' always beatin' up on her. Now come on down here and talk to me on the ground like a man, not a monkey up a tree."

"I ain't no monkey. I'm a man an' a man's got a right to argue wit' his wife if'in he wants. Ain't no'un else's business."

"Ya' cain't hit ya wife. Zeke, that is against the law. But it can all be straightened out if you come on down here, ya hear. Besides, no point in starving when we got a nice venison stew over to the jail for supper."

"Reckon ya' right sheriff. I'm comin' down. Don't shoot." With that announcement, Zeke half climbed, half fell out of the tree at the sheriff's feet.

"Okay. Cuff 'im and book 'im boys," Sheriff Cole stated to the two deputies who had the unsteady man cuffed and began leading him towards the cruiser as they recited a mountainized version of the Miranda act.

The sheriff turned to Casey, "You shouldn't get so close to a stand off like that, young lady. You could get hurt."

"Sheriff Cole, I knew you had it all under control," Casey murmured.

"An' don't go pulling any of that 'Scarlett stuff' on me; I know you better than that by now."

"You're right, Sheriff. But I do thank you for being so 'on the spot' when I needed you."

"Just doin' my job. I was pullin' into Tom's to get your statement just as you pulled out and that varmint hit you."

"Well, whatever. I am grateful. Would it constitute bribery if I bought you a cup of coffee at Nancy's while I give you a statement?"

"Not in the least. Nancy always keeps the pot hot, with a special cup for me and never does charge me. I'll be just the place to sit a spell and get your story. No point writing up a report in a car on a mountain road when I can just as well do it in air conditioned comfort at Nancy's."

After giving the sheriff her statement and assuring Nancy that she was unhurt, Casey drove to the office. Velma Lou was closeted with Mayor Campbell but the conference broke up shortly after Casey settled in at her desk. She managed to look too busy to notice when Dirk, left but Velma Lou wouldn't be put off that way.

She called Casey into her office and shut the door. "I heard all about what happened this morning. I'll understand if you want to get out of the mountains for a while. If you want to go to Atlanta or anywhere, I'll finish up the Memorial Day piece. You can just bring that diary and other material here and take off right away. I know you must be all shook up."

"Whoa," Casey stemmed her cousin's flow of unusually solicitous conversation. "I'm fine. Zeke's in jail. My car's fixed. And I've got a great story of the 'mountain chase' and arrest. The Confederate piece is coming along nicely; and about the dairy, it's so personal. Really like a letter from Granny Weesie to me. I couldn't bear to part with it." She didn't tell her cousin of the strange occurrences whenever she read the old book. Velma Lou would think she was nuts.

"Well, of course, I understand, Honey. But it is a historical document and after all, I am family. I surely would love to take a peek at it one day. Maybe later when you feel better. Why don't you just go on home and take it easy, after you finish the article on Zeke's arrest, of course.

Just before she left the office, Lee called. "Would you care to have a pizza with me and come see what I've been doing with the house? I've got it all restored. The kitchen was the last thing and they finished it, finally. The workmen just left and it looks great. Anyway, they found a bunch of old papers in the walls when they were finishing up and I thought you might like to see them."

"Why, Lee, I thought you were so busy lately you didn't have time for the house or me," she replied in her most honeyed tones. You two timing bastard, she thought but didn't say.

"Well I did have to take care of some family business yesterday, but that's all taken care of now and I have time to spend with the person I really want to see."

Family business! More like funny business! "Sorry, Lee, I have some 'family business' I need to take care of this evening."

"Well, maybe tomorrow." His tone was a bit baffled.

She hung up without another word. If she stayed

on the line much longer, she would tell him just what she thought of men who slept with one cousin and then tried to make time with another.

Back home, she had several "hang up" calls while she worked on the article. After the last one, she briefly considered that Lee was checking on her but decided that wasn't his style. Anyway, he was probably chasing after some other woman. That was his style.

When she finally snuggled into the old four-poster, it was just natural to pick up the dairy. It must be some kind of dream state induced by the smell of the old paper. Either that or she really was losing it. Whatever, it sure beat television for realistic historical drama.

Smokey appeared unusually watchful this evening and settled in at the foot of her bed as she picked up the old book.

Daniel and I are being married today. He's not Jonathan, but he is a good man. He'll make a good husband and father if I am lucky enough to have any children. I wish Lillie would take better care of her beautiful baby. But she and David are always fighting! Always drunk!

Louisa was in the cabin putting the finishing touches on her costume. Her mother sat on the bed with a few stray tears tracing a path down her cheeks. Louisa understood how hard it must be for her parents to lose their baby. Both brothers, Robbie and Matthew, had married shortly after Lillith. Both of the wives were local girls Louisa had known and liked all her life. They had arrived early to help her celebrate. Lillith and David would be in the crowd milling around the front yard also, but Louisa almost wished they wouldn't come. The weather was all any bride could ask. The bright sun made the pink rhododendrons with their deep green leaves that ranged up the mountainside look like a scene in a fancy magazine. The goldenrod was blooming in the valley and the Queen o' the Meadow was just developing its distinctive purple heads atop the waving stalks. In the fields, the sorghum stood tall and straight.

When she descended the steps of the porch, flanked by her parents, Daniel stood waiting out front to greet them. A friend, who was a circuit-riding preacher, had come across the mountains from the booming gold fields of Dahlonega to perform the ceremony. Ma shooed Daniel away. "It ain't lucky for the groom to see the bride on her weddin' day before the ceremony."

Daniel gently reproved his future mother-in-law. "Now, Miz Hatty, you know that superstition is the devil's tool." He turned to help Louisa down the steps. "And a refreshing sight she is, too, in that delightful frock."

"Why thank you, Daniel." She smoothed the blue linen frock. She had worked over it by lantern light many a night to get the full skirt to flow gently and add the tiny touches of embroidered dogwood flowers around the collar and at the hem that swirled around her ankles. It was the kind of dress she wouldn't get to wear often as a preacher's wife. Gingham and flour sacking would be more normal. It wouldn't do to appear to set herself above her husband's parishioners. Daniel pressed something into her hand, a small round pod of buckeye. Tears filled her eyes. She had never considered him particularly romantic, but now she felt there might be a side to her new husband-to-be that she wasn't aware of. She understood the significance. In the mountains, these buckeye pods were considered the symbol of a happy couple. The pods fit together inside the hulls just as a married couple was expected to fit together in their life.

Just behind Daniel was Lillith. She looked as if she had tried to clean up a bit for the occasion, but there was no disguising the fading black eye or the large purple bruise on the side of her face. It was too sad looking at Lillie now. She had been so beautiful as a bride just a little over a year ago. Her baby, Anne, had been born that November and things kept getting worse between her sister and her husband. Now, Lillith looked a dozen years older than her twenty-nine years. She seldom washed, and the body odor mixed with the smell of whiskey on her breath was devastating. She had lost one of her front teeth. She said it had been knocked out in a fall, but Louisa had her suspicions. David was not a gentle man, even when sober. He was seldom sober now.

The house, once Donald's pride, was now becoming ramshackle. It was the baby that broke Louisa's heart most. Poor Anne looked like a tiny angel, with her mother's golden curls and huge green eyes, but she was always dirty and seemed to cringe when either of her parents shouted at her to "mind". At seven months, the tiny mite was under weight and frail. Louisa longed to shelter her little niece, but could do nothing to help her. She vowed that when she and Daniel had a child, it would be so different. She and Daniel had discussed it so often. Daniel said he felt bad for the child but "it was the Lord's will and they just had to accept it".

Privately, Louisa thought "the Lord" had little to do with the raising of her tiny niece. It was Lillie and David's will and no one should have to accept that kind of treatment of a baby.

David was nowhere in sight. Lillith saw the look her sister cast around. "David couldn't come. He was feeling a mite sickly today."

Louisa had a pretty good idea what ailed her brother-in-law but, nonetheless, she was glad of his absence. The baby, Anne, had pulled herself upright and was tugging on her mother's skirt. Lillith ignored the child, who finally gave up and sat down to play in the dirt. Louisa reached down to pat her niece's golden curls. "Hello, Darlin'. How's Aunty Weesie's sweet thing?"

Lillith picked the child up and perched her on her opposite hip. "She'll just get ya all dirty. You do look so pretty. I'm so proud of my baby.....sister. Do be happy." The older woman turned away to hide the rush of tears that filled her once beautiful eyes.

Her brothers greeted her enthusiastically. They had both brought musical instruments; Matt, a fiddle and Robbie, a dulcimer. Daniel disapproved of music, especially fiddling; but as the brothers were just going to play sacred music like Amazing Grace for the ceremony, he allowed that it was acceptable. "As long as it don't lead to reels and other dance tunes. That's the devil's work," he proclaimed.

The ceremony was beautiful. Ma and some of the other women had decorated the yard with masses of rhododendron blooms they had picked in the woods. A few other men got mandolins, banjos and mouth harps out of their wagons and joined the Garrett boys to provide a musical side to her wedding day. Since the groom was not a local man, he had no family nearby to provide an infare Wedding. The Garrett's were going to provide a proper send off for Louisa. Due to the fact of Daniel's calling, the traditional shivaree with all the female relatives banging on pots and hooting outside the young couple's bedroom on the wedding night had been tastefully called off. Her friends had shown their affection by each bringing a layer to add to her wedding stack cake so it stood tall and proud, its apple and molasses filling dripped profusely down the sides.

After the brief ceremony, the group continued to play. They barely skirted the reels and other dance music that the preacher had forbidden. Once or twice, Daniel looked as if he would put a stop to it; but he refrained, knowing his young bride had grown up with music as part of her life as had most of the other guests. As long as no one actually danced, he overlooked the discreet toe tapping. After a rousing rendition of "Shady Grove", the boys enjoined Louisa to join them in a version of "Buffalo Boy". Louisa's clear soprano led "Buffalo Boy". "When we going to get married, married, married? When we going to get married, my dear old buffalo boy?"

Matt replied in his deep tenor, "Well, I guess we'll get married on Sunday, Sunday, Sunday. I guess we'll get married on Sunday, if'en the weather's alright."

Louisa chimed back in with her part. "How you gonna get to the wedding, the wedding, the wedding? How you gonna get to the wedding, my dear old buffalo boy?"

Then the man's answer, "Guess I'll bring the ox cart, the ox cart, the ox cart. Guess I'll bring the ox cart, if'en the weather's alright."

"Why don't you bring the buggy, the buggy, the buggy? Why don't you bring the buggy, my dear old buffalo boy?"

"Cause my chill'en won't fit in the buggy, the buggy, the buggy. My chill'en won't fit in the buggy, even if the weather's alright."

Louisa cast her brother a mock-surprised look. "Didn't know you had any children, children, children. Didn't know you had any children, my dear old buffalo boy."

Matt played straight man. "Oh, yes, I have five children, children, children. Yes, I have five children, maybe six if the weather's alright."

"There ain't going to be no wedding, wedding, wedding. There ain't going to be no wedding, my dear old buffalo boy."

Matt pretended to pull out a wad of bills from his pocket. "But I got 5 million dollars, dollars, dollars. I got 5 million dollars, maybe 6 if the weather's alright."

"When we gonna get married, married, married? When we gonna get married, my dear old buffalo boy?" Louisa finished the rollicking ditty, finally, and almost fell into Daniel's arms in a fit of laughter.

Even Daniel had to admit it was good fun. If fact it was such good fun, they all continued until the sun was peeping over the horizon signaling the start of a new day. The now subdued band ended with the mournful "Barbara Allen".

Perhaps a ballad telling of the death of both bride and groom was a bit somber to play for a wedding, but it was part of the mountain culture brought over by early Scotch-Irish ancestors and adapting over the years to reflect the mountain heritage.

The simple folk music melted into a complicated arrangement by Reba, with a saxophone backup. What was Reba doing here? Who was playing that sax? Casey realized it was her clock radio alarm and she was back in the 21st century. She wondered how Louisa and Daniel worked things out in the nineteenth. Granny has seldom talked about her younger years. Or if she had, it didn't make much impression on a five-year-old.

Well, she'd spent enough time dwelling in the past. It was time to get on with her future. She needed to get to the office and turn in the Confederate Memorial piece and several others she had written. She was especially happy with her piece on Zeke's capture; both from the literary, if you could call the factual piece literature, and the personal. She felt as if she could now safely function with out anyone trying to harm her. Zeke, of course, had insisted he had nothing to do with sabotaging her brakes. His cousin could not be found.

Plus today, she needed to cover a Chamber of Commerce luncheon at Bodine's. She dreaded facing Lee, who would be formally introduced as a new Chamber of Commerce member, but she would have to get through it. She decided she would be cool and polite, but distant. After all, why should she care if her neighbor, who she had only known for a short time, was sleeping with her gorgeous cousin?

The problem was she did care. Of course, she had no intention of getting involved with him or any other man for a long, long time. But a tiny spot in her heart ached. She had felt so comfortable, so protected, with Lee. She had felt sure he was different from Ray. She decided her judgment of men certainly wasn't up to par. After all, she had once trusted Ray. Resolutely, she put all thoughts of Lee out of mind. Never the less she chose her costume for the luncheon very carefully. After rummaging through the closet and discarding three or four outfits as not being up to snuff, she decided on an ecru pants suit with a lime green silk tank top. The slacks fit well enough to show her curves, but were not so tight as to be suggestive. The jacket skimmed her waist and emphasized the soft curves that the clingy top revealed. She slipped into a pair of sandals with just high enough heels to thrust her pelvis forward and slim her ankles.

Velma Lou was pleased with the Zeke story but felt the Confederate story lacked something. She was vague when Casey tried to pin her down as to exactly what she wanted. "Maybe if I took a peek at that famous diary you have, I could give you a better idea. It just seems to be lacking something."

Casey was equally vague about the diary. "It really doesn't have much about the war or Confederate veterans."

As luck would have it, Casey was seated next to Lee at the luncheon. He seemed puzzled by her coolness. After the lunch, the guest began to depart. Lee reached for her arm to keep her at the table with him a moment more. "Have I done something to offend you?"

She replied in her best Southern Magnolia manner. "Why, Darlin', if you want to sleep with

Velma Lou, I just feel I should stay out of the picture."

"Sleep with Velma Lou? Me? I admit, she's beautiful, but so is a forest fire and I wouldn't throw myself into that either. Why on earth would you think that I'm ...involved with her? And for heaven's sake, drop the Scarlett act. It's not you."

"Well, you left the office with her the other day and when I got home, you still weren't back. Then I called her and she was saying a very romantic 'good night' to ...I thought it was you, since you got home just a little while after that." Looking at it now it did all seem like flimsy evidence on which to condemn someone. "I guess I owe you an apology."

Lee laughed. "Honey, if I didn't know better, I'd swear you might be a tiny bit jealous."

"Me? Jealous?" She tried for a laugh, but it didn't come out right. Jealousy implied romance, or love, or something like that. She and Lee were just friends. She tried to convince herself, but suddenly she knew her feelings for the rugged scientist were more than she was acknowledging. *Oh, my God! I'm not ready for a new relationship!* But try as she might, she knew without a doubt, she was in love.

She told Lee about the events of the last few days. "I feel safer now that Zeke's in jail," she concluded.

"This Zeke doesn't sound like he is smart enough to plot and plan. Could there be something else? What about your ex-husband?"

"Ray? No. He's probably happy as a lark chasing young secretaries. He has no reason to bother me."

"Maybe you're right. I just feel uneasy with you all alone in the cabin. Why don't you come stay at my house for a while?"

She would never be able to sort out all these confusing feeling at his house. "No, no, I don't think so."

He didn't push, but Casey could read in his eyes that he didn't consider the matter closed. "Well, at least come over and let me cook you dinner in my newly remodeled kitchen. You can read all those old papers my workmen found inside the wall."

"Okay. How about seven? And should I bring anything?"

"Seven is fine, and just bring yourself."

She hopped in her car with a lighter heart than she had had in a long time. She decided she would run by Ingles and pick up a sinfully rich Black Forest Cake from their bakery department. After a brief stop at the office where she quickly wrote up the Chamber luncheon piece, she headed for home. It was only after she was pulling into her driveway that she realized she had forgotten the cake from the grocery. *I'll rest a bit, then change clothes and run to the store before I go to Lee's*, she promised herself.

As usual Smokey was waiting for her. She considered sweeping and dusting around the cabin, but realized it looked as if it was freshly cleaned. Strange, she thought, she hadn't done much cleaning since she moved into the cabin but it always looked fresh. She had an instant flash of Granny Weesie, wearing her old apron over a faded calico dress, dusting and sweeping when she was a child. Granny had always kept the place spotless. It was almost like she was still around taking care of the place. She shrugged off the absurd notion. *I need a rest. It's been a hectic week.* She replenishing Smokey's food, and was about to lie down when the phone rang.

It was Nancy. They chatted a minute, then Nancy told her why she had called. "I just wanted to let you know I heard Zeke's out on bail. Be careful."

She promised Nancy she would, but she wasn't in the mood to take an old windbag like Zeke too seriously today. She was in a good mood and nothing was going to spoil it. She couldn't resist picking up the old diary. She would just read a few pages before she changed and got dressed for dinner with Lee.

I haven't written in this ol' book in years. Here tis way up in the fall of 90 and I jus gotta get it all out. I promised Lillie I'd take care of her Anne. But it's hard. It's very hard.

Lillith lay very still in the big bed. "Promise me! Promise you'll take lil' Anne. David's no good for her. David ain't no good to anyone not even his own self. He's got a demon on his shoulder and a guilt in his heart that's eatin' him all up."

"Tain't no point talkin' lik' this, Lillie. You're gonna be fine. You'll get better. Maybe Dan could talk to David about his drinkin' an…"

"David is what he is. We all know that. An' I ain't gonna get better. Ther's somethin' eating up my innards. Granny MacLeod cain't help me with none of her herbs an' even the doctor in Dahlonega cain't do nothin'." She changed the subject abruptly, "Ma's getting' all funny in the head since Da died. Claims to see 'im around the place. Says he even still cuts her firewood."

"Dan cuts her firewood when we go visit." Louisa couldn't tell her sister that she, too, had sensed her father's presence in the cabin. "Ma's jus' getting on. She misses Da. It's worse since the boys have gone to Atlanta to live."

"No matter. I want you to raise my girl. Lord knows, I ain't been much of a mother to her but I do love 'er. It's jus' myself I don't like too much. It ain't right me havin' a beautiful child like her an' you not havin' no young'uns at all. Besides she's your…" a fit of coughing stopped the rapid flow of words.

Louisa had the feeling her sister had been about to tell her something important; but when she resumed talking, she seemed to have forgotten what she was going to say. Louisa sat with her sister all that night. In the morning, Lillith Garrett Stuart's troubled life was over. David never came home. Louisa sent the frightened Anne to fetch Daniel and her mother.

Together the two women prepared Lillith's body for burial. Daniel took Anne with him to arrange with Mr. Shook, the carpenter, to make a simple pine box. Then he went to the church and rang the bell 38 times, one for each year Lillith had spent on this earth. Neighbors began arriving with dishes of food. They came for my sake and my mother's. Few in the village had liked Lillith.

David arrived later in the afternoon. He was drunk. Ma told him of his wife's death, since I could barely stand to be near him. It didn't seem to pierce the alcoholic fog that befuddled his brain almost constantly nowadays. He went upstairs to sleep it off and when he came down near dark, he appeared sobered. He sat near Lillith's coffin for a long time, then he disappeared. He took no clothes or supplies with him, so everyone assumed he would turn up for the funeral next day but he didn't. The weather fit the funeral mood. It rained torrents and lightning split the sky. The tall pines waved furiously, threatening to upend their shallow roots and crash into the mourners.

The mountains seemed gray in the mists and the red earth was slippery with the deluge. As Daniel and a few of the men folks dug the grave, the red clay poured back into the hole. It seemed as if the earth of Bluejay didn't want to receive Lillith's body anymore than she had wanted to live upon it in life. Lillith had long ago given up trying to leave the mountains. Now she never would.

Louisa sighed. She loved little Anne and Dan spoiled the child terribly. She tried to capture her feelings as she wrote it all into the old diary.

With David gone, there was no longer any question as to whether I would take Anne home with me now. She was so like Lillith in appearance, it was like havin a miniature of my sister to remind me of her. I had loved Lillith. The bond between us had always been strong. However, I didn't like her, if that makes any sense. I never forgot the night I had followed her to the barn and found Jonathan dead. Little had been heard about his wife and child after they left the mountains. Daniel had heard that they had gone to Atlanta, where Miz Carley had died a short time later. A distant relative named Schmidt had taken in the little boy. Daniel had not heard anything else about him after that. We would have been happy to take the child and raise him, but Miz Carley had wanted nothing more to do with Bluejay after the tragedy she had endured here. So I had no child to mother until now. Anne was beautiful. But she was so like Lillith.

I wondered often what Lillith had been about to tell me that last night, but put it aside. I would never find out. My sister was gone. All that was left of her was contained in the small blond girl child I tried so hard to understand. Her mother had been dead nigh on to three months now and the child is yet to show any sign of grief. Perhaps it's like Dan says, "Some people hide their feelings while others wear them on their sleeve. It don't mean one feels any less strongly than the other. The Lord made us all different." Course, Dan dotes on that youngun. He couldn't see anything wrong with her no matter what she does.

We're gitting ready to go down the mountain a piece to my cousin Charlie Dugan's house for a sorghum harvest party. The McDougal's just up the holler would be there. Thank heavens, Dan has mellowed a bit about the music. They'll be fiddling and picking tonight. An dancin. Course, Dan still won't allow me to dance. But at least, I can sit on the porch and listen to the music. It takes me back to all the nights we had everybody over for pickin and singin. Da, Robbie and Matt would make those fiddles and banjoes ring, and Lillie would flirt and dance with all the boys, and I would romp around with the other younguns and suck on the sorghum stalks and make myself sick on the taffy and popcorn balls we made from the sweet syrup. Well, enough reminiscin. Time to get ready and try to get that child in a clean dress.

Louisa laid the book aside and called, "Anne. Anne, come on in here and get dressed."

The child materialized, silently as always. "I'm right here, Aunt Weesie. Do I have a new dress to wear?"

"No, child, you just got a new dress last month. It's perfectly good for visiting relatives."

"I want a new dress! Mary Beth McCormick has a new one every week. I'm prettier than her, so I should have a new dress, too." The child stamped her foot and shook her golden curls.

"Mary Beth's dad is the president of the bank. Your uncle is just a poor preacher."

"If Uncle Dan knew how much I wanted a new dress, he'd get me one. I want the one they have in the window at Alexander's." Another bout of foot stomping.

"Hush your whining. Put on this dress. It's perfectly good. Besides, the one in Alexander's window is way too old for you. It's a woman's dress."

"It's pretty and red. I want it." Anne folded her arms across her chest, which was already showing signs of blossoming into womanhood.

Daniel arrived at that moment. "What's the problem, sweetheart?"

The child threw herself into his arms. "I hate having to wear old raggedy dresses when everybody else has pretty new ones. And she won't get me any new ones. You will, won't you, Uncle Dan?" Anne looked at her uncle with tears sparkling on her long lashes.

Daniel looked at Louisa over the golden curls. "Can't we squeeze the budget a bit and get her something new and pretty next week?"

Louisa didn't remind her husband that she hadn't had anything new in several years. "I'll pick up some material and make her a new dress next week."

Anne looked triumphantly at Louisa and reached for the dress in her aunt's hand. "Oh, thank you, Uncle Dan! I love you. I won't mind wearing this old thing when I know I'm getting a new one soon." She retreated into the bedroom to dress, tears all forgotten for the moment.

Louisa laid her head on her husband's shoulder. "You know you spoil her. All she thinks of are new clothes. I don't think she cares a bit for either of us. Just what we can do for her."

He patted his wife's back gently. "She's had such a terrible life. Neither of her parents noticed her most of the time and then when they did, they just bought her something new and forgot her again while they fought or lost themselves in the bottle. It's just going to take time for the child to adjust to a normal family."

When they reached the Dugan cabin, huge clouds of smoke arose into the darkening sky. The stripped cane was being run through a grinder to squeeze out every drop of the juice. A mule plodding in an endless circle powered the grinder. Occasionally, one of the children would stop the animal to offer a small apple or dried handful of corn. As the syrup squirted out between the grinder stones, it was filtered as it flowed down into a huge open trough. The fire was set at the top of the trough so the juice boiled only at the upper end of the copper-bottomed pan. The men were hard at work skimming the greenish foam off the top of the trough nearest the bottom end. The cooked amber syrup was being funneled into a oak barrel. The smell was heavenly.

On the porch, the infectious rhythm of Shady Grove was issuing from a group of men with assorted instruments. Charlie Dugan played the dulcimer. He was seated on a low stool to compensate for the fact that he had lost most of his leg in the war. It didn't slow down his booming baritone. It didn't slow him down in other ways either. His wife, Addie, looked like she was pretty far along in this, her eighth pregnancy. Louisa thought she looked a bit pale. She was at least forty and having a baby at that age was never easy. Living here, where there was no doctor for miles around made it that much worse. Daniel went over to join the men at the trough and Anne joined the children busy pulling taffy. Louisa joined the crowd on the porch.

Charlie's soft dulcimer was overshadowed as Leon Campbell led off on his fiddle with a toe-tapping version of "Turkey in the Straw". By now, some of the younger folks had begun clogging on the hard packed dirt in front of the cabin. By the time the band switched to a reel and the dancers had squared off, Louisa was aware that Addie was having problems. She beckoned the other woman into the kitchen. "Is the baby due soon?"

Addie shook her head. "Not for a coupla more weeks." She grimaced in pain, "But I think this 'un is impatient. He's not gonna wait 'til he's due. He must want to join the party."

"Want me to tell Charlie to git Granny MacLeod to help you birth this 'un?"

"No! No, no point in tellin' Charlie. Men folks ain't no good at birthing a baby, jus' at startin' one. Granny is gone across the mountain to Dahlonega to visit her kin. You gotta help me this time."

"Me?" Louisa tried to think of anyone more experienced in the crowd outside. No use, everyone out there was either too young to have had much experience with birthin' or too giddy to be trusted delivering a baby. "I reckon it's gotta be me. Come on, let's get you in the bedroom."

The birth took less than an hour and was much easier than Louisa had expected, given Addie's age. Charlie was thrilled with his new son, which the proud parents named Luke but vowed to call "Sweety" in honor of his arrival in the midst of a sorghum grinding party. Addie and the new baby didn't rejoin the crowd out front, but the rest of the party continued until another unusual episode disrupted it and dissipated the festive atmosphere.

It was about an hour after the unexpected birth. The band was playing "Turkey in the Straw". Louisa and Daniel were sitting quietly near the back of the porch. They were just about ready to leave. Louisa was exhausted but exhilarated with her new role as midwife. "It was like seeing God's handwork in action!" She explained to Daniel. She knew she would eagerly assist the next time any of the local women needed a midwife. Granny McLeod was getting up in years.

The band stopped suddenly. Everybody seemed to stop talking and a deadly quiet fell over the gathering. David had returned. A young woman wearing a tight red dress accompanied him. Her hair was a bright yellow and she was wearing rouge and lip paint. "Evening, Charlie," David said. He appeared relatively sober.

Charlie and the entire group stared. "Don't recall invitin' you, David Stuart. For a man what cain't even come to his own wife's funeral to show up uninvited an' haulin' a strumpet behind 'im at decent folk's grindin' party, well, I reckon' you jus' ain't welcome here."

The insults didn't seem to faze David at all. "Marcie and I just came to pick up my little girl. We got our own party. Don't need any of your hospitality."

Daniel walked over to his brother-in-law. "This is family business, Charlie. David and I have some things to discuss. If you'd rather I took David to my place, I will."

Charlie gave David another hard look. He didn't even acknowledge the woman with him. "Daniel Murcott, you can talk to anybody you want at my house anytime you want. But when you finished with that piece of garbage, he can just hightail it off my property and never set foot on it ag'in. His brother was a fine man. But him, he just insults Donald Stuart's memory by living and breathing when his brother is buried in the cold ground all these years. I reckon' he knows more about how he got there than me or any other decent folks." He picked up his fiddle and began to play "Dixie".

David ignored the insults and motioned his brother-in-law out of the way. "I'm just here to get

Anne. I appreciate you carin' for her, but I'm home now and gonna take what's mine."

"Don't you think Anne might be better off staying with us for a while?" Daniel queried.

"She's mine and I'm taking her home now. Anne? Anne where are you?"

The child silently sidled between her father and her uncle. "Will you buy me that new dress in Alexander's window, Daddy?"

"Sure, Anne. I'll buy you whatever you want." With a triumphant look over his shoulder, David picked up the child and headed for his buckboard.

Anne waved over his shoulder. "Bye, Uncle Dan. I'll come over and see you soon."

The party was over. As Daniel and Louisa drove home behind the plodding horse, Daniel was as near tears as Louisa had ever seen him. "It's the Lords will. We can't question His will," he murmured over and over.

Louisa tried to offer comfort. But she couldn't forget the child's face when she wheedled the new dress from her father. She, too, was heartsick but for different reasons. She had promised her sister to look after her child, but in her heart she was happy the child was gone from their home. The wagon wheels seemed to be repeating, "It's best. It's best. It's best."

"Casey? It's Lee. Are you okay?" The repetition of the wagon wheels turning over the red clay road was replaced by a voice from the present. She opened her eyes to find her handsome neighbor leaning over her, concern evident on his face. "I called and you didn't answer. I walked up and pounded on the door but still no answer. Your body was cool and I couldn't wake you up. You frightened me. It was like you were in some kind of trance. Are you okay?"

The thing she wanted most was to slide over and let this gentle man join her in the old oak bed. She wanted his hands on her naked body, not just touching her face. Instead, she jumped up. "I'm okay but there is something that has been happening lately. I need to tell you about it."

"Oh my God, are you ill? Is something wrong?"

"No. No, it's nothing wrong exactly." She pondered on a simple way of telling someone you have been doing time travel. There was no simple way. "It's complicated. Let's have a cup of tea and I'll try to explain."

"If you're feeling up to it, I have dinner ready and

a bottle of wine chilled at my place."

"Oh, what time is it?" She glanced at the radio clock. It was 7:20. "I was going to pick up a dessert..." She noticed the strange look on Lee's face. "What's wrong?"

"Look on your kitchen counter."

She did. She looked at Lee, but he was staring at the freshly baked, newly frosted, perfect chocolate cake resting on one of Granny Weesie's favorite antique Blue Ridge Plates. Could some one have baked it while she slept? She looked around the kitchen for signs of an intruder. No one was in the kitchen except Smokey, sitting by his dish licking his paws. Anyway, intruders didn't bake chocolate cakes. In fact, no one she knew could bake a cake that perfect. No one, except Granny Weesie. " I must be losing my mind," she concluded.

"I've heard of people doing all kinds of amazing things while they were sleepwalking. But to bake a cake like that and then clean up any trace of preparation...?" Lee stepped over to the stove. "The oven isn't even warm. Are you sure you didn't have someone bake this and brought it home with you earlier?"

"Let's get out of here and go up to your place. Would you put that in a carrier for me while I dress? There is a Tupperware carrier in the bottom of that cabinet."

Alone in her room, she tried to make some sense out of recent events. She couldn't find any explanation in modern logical thought. Granny Weesie and her contemporaries would have accepted them as part of the magic of the mountains. Spirits and "the sight" were part of the Scotch, Irish and Cherokee heritage of this ancient Appalachian culture. Her culture. Her heritage.

She quickly slipped into a pair of jeans and an

Alan Jackson tee and returned to the kitchen where Lee had the cake firmly encased in Tupperware.

"Ready?" he asked.

They left the ancient cabin to Smokey who continued his untroubled grooming ritual.

On Lee's porch, they both had to spend several minutes petting the puppies before they could enter the house through the back door. Lee explained that he let them inside sometimes but was still working on their "manners" so they had to stay on the porch today. Casey gazed at the kitchen in approval. The new kitchen embodied the best of both worlds. The exposed beams of the ceiling were left intact, their mellow heart of pine gleamed softly in the light of the three wide windows overlooking a spectacular view of the valley and the mountains on the opposite side of the town. The window treatments consisted of a valance of white with a green twining vine pattern and vertical blinds that could be drawn for privacy. The blinds were now fully open to take advantage of the view. The wall with the huge fireplace was a solid backdrop of flat stonework to set off a superb collection of black iron pots and pans and other unique antique kitchen utensils. The floor was still a softly patinaed oak. At first glance, the stove appeared to be a huge black and copper wood-burning contraption. On closer inspection, it revealed itself as a modern gas stove created deliberately to blend into this type of kitchen. Set like an island in the middle of the vast room, with working counter space on both sides, it dominated the room. Above it hung a copper hood with hooks for utensils containing a lot of the larger black iron pots. The rest of the kitchen was pure twenty-first century, from a copper fronted side-by-side refrigerator to the marble counters and the natural pine wood cabinets. Lots of hanging plants set off the soft sunshine colored walls

"Oh, what a magnificent kitchen," Casey exclaimed. "Cooking in here would make you feel like a celebrity chef on television.

She perched gingerly on the edge of one of the oak chairs and fingered the pale blue Mason jar Lee had used for a vase to contain the mass of Black-Eyed-Susans adorning the table.

"Thank you. Cooking has always been my hobby. I like modern appliances but I couldn't bear to sacrifice the old fashioned charm of this room."

"What is that fabulous aroma?" Casey queried.

"Well, it could be the pork medallions or the saffron rice but it's probably the seven-grain bread in my bread machine over there." He pointed to the small white machine sitting inconspicuously in a corner of one counter.

"Oh my God! I have died and gone to heaven." Casey let out an exaggerated sigh and sank back more comfortably into the chair. "Granny Weesie used to make some bread like that. Of course she did it in the oven, but she used to get that stone ground flour from a mill that ground it special. I would never have remembered it all those years ago except this smells just like it. Or at least as close as a five year old's recollections can be trusted."

Lee smiled at her approval. He went over and began dislodging the bread from the machine. "I cheated with the machine but I did buy the flour and grains from a mill over on Gainesville Highway." He put the bread in a rustic basket and covered it with a white napkin. "If you will get the butter, I think we are just about ready." He set out some heavy brown earthenware plates and silverware. "The wine is chilling in that." He pointed to a matching bowl. "I didn't have anything fancy but it is big enough to do the job." He loosened the cork and poured them each a glass. "The rest of the meal is in the oven keeping warm." He turned to get it.

"Let me help you get it. You have everything so organized." Casey jumped up to help. She spun around and almost crashed into him. With half filled wineglasses in each hand, he closed his arms around her or she would have fallen. The casual embrace did more damage than a fall would have. Her heart pounded so loudly she was sure he could feel it through her tee shirt and his thin cotton shirt.

They both stepped back at the same moment. "Sorry, I didn't realize you were right behind me. I just wanted to help." Casey tried to cover her embarrassment. She couldn't look in his face. However as she glanced downward, she couldn't help but notice his body had had a strong reaction to her touch as well. His snug Levi's couldn't conceal it. She felt the color rising in her face.

"I'll just start slicing the bread," he murmured, turning towards the counter. "You go ahead and set the table."

After the meal was completed, Casey poured herself another glass of the apple-flavored wine. "This stuff is really good. What kind is it?"

Lee picked up the simple green bottle with its cream color label. "It's called Georgia White Reisling. Comes from Habersham Winery over in Nacoochee Village near Helen. Have you ever been over to the village there?"

"No," she replied.

"I'll take you one day. They have a complete old time village replicated there. Aside from getting great local wines, it's a fun trip. We can stop in Helen and eat at one of those little German themed restaurants overlooking the Chattoochee River."

"I'd love it. I guess I have stalled long enough. At least a few glasses built my courage up to tell you about what's been happening."

"Casey, I hope you won't ever be afraid to tell me anything. You know I'll help you any way I can." He reached over to touch her, but drew back at the last minute.

"This is going to sound crazy. Hell, I think it's crazy and it's happening to me. That's the problem. I know it's impossible but I also know it's happening." She reached over and put a finger across his lips as he started to interrupt. "No, just hear it all out before you say anything." She told him everything beginning with finding the dairy.

After she finished, Lee gulped the last of his wine. "I know that's what you think is happening…"

"It is happening!" she interrupted. No 'think' about it. I 'see' things only Weesie would have known. The sights, the smells, it's all happening. Added to that, I 'know' things that only existed in my great grandmother's mind. Even things that I don't 'witness'. I 'recall' her Christmases in the mountains. I 'remember' getting an orange stuffed in my stocking one Christmas morning. I 'know' what it feels like to go out to the well on a snow-covered morning to draw water. I 'remember' threading those old fashioned beans they called Leather Britches and hanging them in the kitchen to dry. That and a million other things I, as Casey, never experienced. How can you explain that?"

"That's just my point," he continued softly. "Maybe these are things your granny told you as a child. Maybe they are coming out now because you are in her house. Maybe because you're under stress. Any number of reasons repressed memories come to the front of a person's mind. It doesn't mean you're crazy or anything."

"No! Lee, I was just five when she died. Can you picture an old lady, a sweet loving great grandmother telling a child about murder or miscarriages or an adulterous older sister? No way. I saw those things myself as they happened to my great grandmother back in the nineteenth century. I was there!" She laid her head on the table and began to sob softly.

Lee was at her side at once. He knelt by her chair and enveloped her in his arms. "Please darling, don't cry. It's not that bad. I believe you really are experiencing something. I just want to help find out what and why." He stroked her hair and pulled her towards him.

The warmth and comfort of a strong male body, Lee's body, was something Casey could no longer resist. She turned to him and snuggled into his powerful embrace. His firm lips sought her tear-wet lips. The kisses began gently, offering comfort. Rapidly they deepened into something entirely different. Her mouth opened to admit his probing tongue. She returned the openmouthed kiss with equal fervor. His hands roamed from her hair to her breasts. Casey strained against him and worked one hand beneath his untucked shirt; the feel of muscular bare flesh excited her even more. Her reaction only added fuel to the already out of control flame. His hands struggled to undo her bra. She pushed his hands away and undid the clasp. Her breasts tumbled into his hands. She tugged the tee shirt over her head and tossed it away. She popped several of the buttons on his shirt as she strove to feel their bare flesh merging.

He scooped her up in his arms. "Not here. I want you in my bed," he groaned.

"Oh yes!" she gasped. "Bed. But now. Quick."

He never made it upstairs. They fell in a panting heap on the butter soft leather sofa in the next room.

She wriggled out of her jeans as he caressed her breast with one hand and loosened his own jeans with the other. His erection was velvet soft and hard as steel. His fingers found the center of her womanhood as his mouth sucked urgently on first one breast then the other. She was wet and ready for him almost instantly.

Afterwards, Casey lay snuggled next to his hard body on the sofa, now slick and wet from their frantic coupling. "Oh, Lee, I never intended..."

He laughed softly. "Me neither, darling, but I'm not sorry it happened. Are you?"

She thought it over for just a minute. "No. No, I'm not. I wasn't ready to get involved. I don't know where we're going with this, but I'm not sorry about tonight."

He kissed her lips softly. "I hope I never make you sorry about making love with me." He looked a bit sheepish, "I am sorry I wasn't prepared. I will be next time."

"Prepared?" Then she understood. "I'm not a blushing teenager. I'm not likely to get pregnant with one episode of unprotected sex."

"Pregnant! Oh, my god! I wasn't thinking about that. I was just ... Well, you know. You hear so much about 'safe sex'. I guess I'm not used to playing the dating game again. I was married for so long. You are safe that way. There wasn't anyone but Carole."

She laughed. "I guess I'm out of style, too. There was just Ray and towards the end, we never had sex anymore. I guess we're both safe on that point." The fact that he had said "the next time" gave her a nice warm feeling. It wasn't just a casual incident for him either.

His soft kiss was becoming more intense. "I didn't mean to rush things. I just wanted you so bad," he murmured against her lips. "I've got a good idea."

Her hand brushed between his legs. "I know. I feel your 'idea' and it sure is good."

"You keep touching me like that, you'll never get

to see my bedroom. Come on." He took her hand and led her towards the stairs.

"But my clothes. I'm naked." she protested.

"That's great. You don't need any clothes in my bed. In fact, clothes would just be a hindrance to what I have in mind."

"Sex maniac," she giggled as she followed him up the stairs.

"This time we can take our time and enjoy this the way it was meant to be enjoyed." And they did.

Much later lying in the darkened room, Casey began to think about what had happened. Things were moving too fast for her. Lee had been an attentive lover. They had talked long into the night. She was aware he expected her to stay with him for the rest of the night. She knew he was no Ray, but was she really ready to become that involved? She knew they were both tremendously attracted to one another. Had been since that first time their hands touched in the parking lot at the Experiment Center. She gazed out the huge window; just a few lights still twinkled on the mountainside the window faced. The moon was immense. In fact it looked almost like daylight. Her house was hidden behind the huge cluster of Kudzu-covered underbrush and dead trees that she now knew was the site of the old barn. They had never really gotten into that whole mess either. But it was happening. She was getting glimpses into the past. No matter what explanation Lee's scientist's mind used to try to rationalize her experiences, she knew without a doubt she was "seeing" a true vision of things that had happened. Suddenly she was seized with an overwhelming need to be in her own bed. Granny Weesie's bed.

She got up and tiptoed downstairs to locate her discarded clothing, dressed in the moonlight and slipped out the kitchen door. She didn't need a flashlight. The moon would guide her home. Fortunately the dogs didn't bark when she came out. They just gave her a sleepy look and settled back into their beds in the corner of the porch.

As she approached the cabin, Smokey materialized out of the night and began weaving in and out between her feet. "Stop it, Smokey, you're going to trip me," she commanded. Of course the cat, like cats everywhere, paid no attention. "Stop," she repeated more firmly this time. As she mounted the cabin steps, a dark figure rushed from her front door. The figure stampeded down the steps, knocking her to the ground. She wasn't sure how long she lay unconscious in the dirt but it could not have been long. She heard a car start and speed down her driveway. She tried to regain her feet but her ankle wouldn't support her weight. Smokey crouched near her. He licked her sore ankle with his rough tongue. "You were trying to keep me from going in the cabin, weren't you, old boy." She petted the soft fur. Smokey meowed. "I guess you just want me to get you some cat food." She struggled to drag herself to the handrail and used it to support her weight as she slowly ascended the stairs. Her assailant had turned off the lights both on the porch and inside as he flew out of the cabin to make his escape.

It seemed like hours, but must have only been minutes before she gained the haven of her sofa. She reached for the phone and called Lee's number by the light of the dial. She couldn't bear to try to make it back to the light. Nothing ever sounded so good as Lee's sleepy "Darling, what's wrong? Where are you?"

He was by her side impossibly fast, hitting the switch and flooding the room with light as he entered. "Oh, my God! What happened? Why didn't you wake me if you needed to come home? Why didn't you stay with me?"

Mutely, she pointed to her now swollen ankle. "Oh, Lee. He pushed me down the stairs. My ankle. It hurts." For the first time, the state of the cabin hit her. "He destroyed my cabin. I had just gotten it back in order from that last break in. Ohooo," she wailed.

Lee held her with one hand and dialed 911 with the other. "Shush. You'll be all right. I'll take care... No operator, I'm talking to a... neighbor. She's been attacked and her house broken into. Send someone to look for whoever did this." " No an ambulance won't be necessary, I'm taking her to the hospital myself." "I don't care if she needs to answer any questions. Talk to her at the hospital." He slammed the receiver down and rushed to her side.

"Lee," she moaned, "I can't get to the hospital. It hurts to walk."

"You're not walking, darling. These your car keys?" He indicated the keys sitting on top of the pile the intruder had probably dumped from her purse.

She nodded and he swooped her into his arms, rushed downstairs and gently deposited her in the passenger seat of her car. They both noticed the putrid smell at the same time. She shrugged. "Smokey probably got so scared he had an accident."

Lee wouldn't leave her until the doctor in the emergency room demanded that he get out so he could examine the patient or he would move on to someone who needed him more.

When the nurse wheeled Casey from the examining cubical with her sprained ankle sturdily bandaged, Lee was waiting on one of the hard vinyl covered chairs. He wasn't alone. Sheriff Cole sat in the next chair.

"Morning, Ms. Carlson. Your ankle feeling better?"

"As long as I don't put any weight on it, it's not

too bad. It just throbs. Do you think it was Zeke that broke into the cabin?"

"No ma'am. I don't."

"But who else would do a thing like that. He tore up the whole place. It's a mess. It's a lot worse than my ankle. You don't know how that makes me feel. Somebody in my house! Touching my things! It's got to be Zeke. I reported him last time he did this. You let him out, didn't you? I want him caught and locked back up."

"It ain't Zeke," the sheriff repeated.

Casey could feel the tinge of hysteria in her voice but she couldn't help it. "He's my worst problem. He has been harassing me for weeks. He threatened me. He tried to kill me. He…"

"I wouldn't say any more, Ms. Carlson. Zeke is still your biggest problem, but he didn't break into your cabin."

"Why do you keep saying it wasn't him? How can you be so sure? Did you catch whoever it was?"

"Nope. We didn't catch anybody but we did find Zeke on your property."

"Well, there. That settles it." Casey replied, but the look in the sheriff's eyes told her it was a long way from settled.

"We found Zeke alright, but he was dead."

Too late, Casey recalled all the reasons she had just given the sheriff why she though the intruder was Zeke. She realized that for a lawman, they all added up to a good motive for murder. Before she could blurt out, "I didn't kill him," Lee interrupted. "How did he die?"

"We won't know for sure until the coroner is finished." The sheriff let his eyes wonder from Casey to Lee. "I don't suppose either of you folks have any idea how Ms. Carlson's worst enemy got into her septic tank?"

Casey was happily surprised when Sheriff Cole didn't take her straight to the station for questioning. Instead they sat in the bare hospital waiting room while he listened to her explanation of where she had been for most of the night and the proceeding day. He suggested again that the perpetrator was looking for a specific item and didn't find it the first time because he got scared off, so he came back and began in the bedroom which he hadn't had chance to search the previous time. When Zeke was blamed for the first break-in, it emboldened the thief to return and try again to find what ever it was he wanted.

Casey couldn't think of anything valuable she had. But the sheriff suggested she consider something that might not be valuable in appearance but could be some type of collector's item or antique. He asked if she had bought anything at a flea market or yard sale that was very old. Casey couldn't think of any thing that might fit that category except the old diary, and it was only of interest to her because of her ancestors.

Lee wanted her to go to his house and rest but

Casey insisted he take her home. "I need to call Velma Lou and then I need to find out if anything is missing at home. Sheriff Cole said to get him a list. I also need to see what my insurance will cover about breakage."

"I already called Velma Lou. She was duly concerned. Told me to tell you to take a few days off to rest your ankle. She says the invitation to stay at her place is still open. I told her you would be safe at my place. Anyway, remember, the sheriff told you your septic system would be 'unavailable for the rest of the day' while they examine it and have it all pumped to see if any evidence is there." He grinned. "Look at the bright side; you're getting a free pumping courtesy of the county."

Casey grimaced, "Ugh! What a place to have to search for evidence. But I just want to check on things. Take me there first and then I'll go to your place like a good little girl. I'll even prop my ankle up and take a nap. I didn't get much sleep last night," she reminded him.

"Okay. I'll take you there just long enough to grab a few necessities and then it's my house and bed for you. That's 'bed' as in sleep, not sex."

The Dailey's Septic System truck was the first thing they noticed in Casey's yard. Just past it, some yellow crime scene tape was visible. The cabin didn't rate the tape but it was obvious the detectives had dusted for fingerprints and searched the house for possible clues related to Zeke's untimely demise. Added to the destruction the intruder had created, the grimy fingerprint powder didn't improve the house's condition or Casey's disposition.

She retrieved an old cane of Granny's from the closet where she had stored it when she just couldn't bring herself to throw it away. Lee tried to get her to sit but she had to see for herself. Last night's devastation was more apparent in daylight. The intruder had dumped the contents of all the drawers in heaps on the floor. It wasn't just limited to the bedroom that the sheriff had suggested as the main target. Food items had been flung from the cabinet to spill among the broken crockery on the floor. Granny's Cheshire Cat pot lay on the floor amidst the carnage; its tail and grin unbroken, the rest unsalvageable. Casey sank into one of the kitchen chairs and buried her face in her hands for several minutes. She would not cry. Not again. It wouldn't help, she told herself sternly.

Then she hobbled into the bedroom. The diary had been laying on the nightstand when she left with Lee last night. It was not there now. Smokey was curled in the bed undisturbed by the damage in the room. He opened first one amber eye, then the next. He yawned and stretched, then padded over to his mistress for the obligatory petting. Afterwards instead of heading for the kitchen and his food bowl, he curled up on the floor just next to the loose board where the diary had laid for so many years. On impulse, Casey bent and pressed the end of the board. It raised up a bit. Lee bent down and removed it. Sure enough, there was the diary in its original hiding place. "I didn't put it there last night. Don't you remember? It was on the table," Casey whispered.

"It was when I went into the kitchen to get that carrier. Remember, you needed to change clothes, but are you sure you didn't...." Lee let the rest of the sentence drift. Casey's stare spoke volumes. "I never heard of a burglar hiding something. Could one of the deputies have replaced it?"

Casey didn't even deign to answer and after a moment, Lee muttered. "I guess that's not likely."

Thoughtfully, Casey took out a blue overnight bag. She placed the book in the bottom and filled it with a change of clothes and a comfortable sleeping tee. A few toiletries from the bathroom and her makeup bag completed her packing. On impulse, she picked up the faded old quilt which had also been thrown on the floor and put it on top of the pile. She turned to Lee. "Would you see if there is any cat food left in the kitchen and fill Smokey's bowl?"

He left her sitting in the disarrayed bedroom while he took care of Smokey's needs.

After Lee settled her into his bed with a pitcher of sweet tea, he left her to rest while he made a quick run to the Experiment Station to pick up some work he could do at home. For the first time, Casey was able to appraise the room where they had made such passionate love. Was it just last night? It seemed ages ago. She felt comfortable here but she reminded herself not to get too dependent on any man. Still, it was nice to have a shoulder to lean on at times like this.

She cast an appraising glance around the room. The walls were the same sunshine color as the kitchen and the furniture was either genuine oak antiques or good reproductions. There was a large oval woven rag rug on the heart of pine floor. The bed was large and high, with rounded oak posts at all four corners, and what felt like a soft feather mattress covered with an obviously new patchwork quilt.

She picked up the diary and began to read. It was just words on old paper. Casey realized she needed more. Just reading the book would not transport her. Something was missing. Carefully she hobbled over to the dresser and retrieved the faded quilt she had grabbed on an impulse when she left the cabin. Back in bed, covered with the quilt, the magic began to work.

All these years wishin for a youngun an now I'm pregnant. Pregnant for the first time at forty one. How

*am I going to get through this with Dan so sick an all.
I been delivering babies all these years, I know how
bad it is when the mother is old for the first un.*

Louisa washed her hands at the basin and went to
check on Daniel. He wasn't doing well. Last winter,
he had caught a cold visiting Old Granny McLeod. It
just wouldn't go away. She had tried all the remedies.
It was the curse of the mountain people. The cold and
damp seemed to settle in the lungs and give them a
fever that would not heal. She had tried putting onions
fried in bacon grease on his chest. She had given him
turpentine mixed with sugar water. When he was at
his worst, she had even administered a concoction
made by heating moonshine and honey together.
Nothing had worked. He stirred when she laid a hand
on his forehead

"I want to get up," he murmured. "There's so
much I need to do and I never feel up to any of it
anymore."

"Hush," Louisa soothed. "I've got some news
that'll make you feel better. How would you like a
baby?"

His rheumy eyes brightened. "Really! But you're
not so young. Will it be alright?"

"Of course, don't I deliver all the babies
hereabouts? I know what to do. I won't have a bit of
trouble," Louisa lied.

"I just hope I live to see it. Picture that, a baby of
our own after all this time."

"Of course, you'll live to see it. You'll be running
around braggin' like any proud daddy." She hoped
this wasn't another lie.

"Get me another dose of that nasty concoction
you call medicine. I've got to get well now."

But Daniel Murcott, husband and father to be,
wasn't destined to see his child. Three weeks later,
when a late March snow still blanketed the land,

Louisa arose just after dawn and set a fire in the big wood stove. She began mixing dough and rolling out biscuits for the morning meal. After putting them into the oven, she poured two cups of coffee and took them into the bedroom to awaken Daniel. In just those few minutes, his gentle soul had departed.

The funeral day was a bright and crisp. Except for the mountain peaks, the snow was melted. The dogwood trees were trying to put out new leaves. Tiny green sprigs of grass were poking upward from the hard red soil of the cemetery. The little creek running behind the church was gurgling as the last of its ice melted. The valley and its surrounding mountains were about to continue their ancient cycle of rebirth. Even Louisa's body, so long barren, was now engaged in producing a new life. Only Daniel was no longer part of that cycle. Daniel and the other residents of the small church yard, David, her father, Lillith and Jonathon. Her thoughts turned to the man she had once loved with a pure heart. Strange, now she could barely remember Jonathan's features but the face of her dear Daniel was locked in her heart. She had been a good wife to him but she always felt a little bit guilty about the part of her she had always reserved for the memory of her first love. Strange, she felt so at peace about that small secret now. Perhaps Daniel had known and understood better than she gave him credit for. Suddenly she realized that Daniel was not gone from the rebirth cycle. In the tiny life she carried below her heart, he would live again just as Anne carried a part of Lillith and she herself carried her mother's and father's essence. Even Jonathan had left a part of himself in the little boy now adopted and bearing another man's name. Only David had left nothing of himself behind. For some reason, that made her sadder than even the fact that Daniel would not be here to greet his child in a few months.

Louisa had finished mopping the puncheon floors of the rectory early on the Saturday before Easter. The new preacher, a man named Charles Duffy, was due to arrive with his family this afternoon. It didn't bother Louisa that she was leaving the home where she had spent many contented years with Daniel. She was returning to the home of her childhood. Her mother was growing feebler and it was only right that Louisa should be there to care for her. The child would be born in September, and it seemed right that it would arrive in the same cabin that its mother had. That was the way of life in the mountains, Parents cared for their children; then children cared for their parents. It was the natural order of things. It wasn't right to leave the place of your birth. Plants never did as well when you pulled up the roots and planted them in a different kind of soil. Same with people, at least mountain people.

She had packed her things in two barrels. She had never had a loom or spinning wheel of her own. Instead she had used the ones at her parent's cabin when she needed to make thread or clothing. Her belongings weren't many, considering the years she had spent here, but they were in the old wagon. All she had to do was hitch up Able, their old mule, and go back to the cabin. She waited for the new preacher before she set out for her old home. She had set a pot of stew simmering on the stove so his wife would not have to cook when she first arrived. Other neighbors had dropped in during the day with small gifts of food for their new preacher and to pass the time with Louisa a bit before heading back to finish their own chores.

Hattie Garrett greeted her daughter at the door and walked with her to the lean-to they used for a barn while Louisa unhitched Able. "I was just tellin' your da about your new baby." The years had not been kind to her mother. Hattie was hunched and wizened with arthritis. She had the same kind of blood spitting cough that had carried Daniel away so rapidly. With Hattie, it was a slower process but would reach the same conclusion before long. Daniel had what was called "Galloping Consumption", but her mother's was just as deadly.

"That's nice, Ma. How is he feeling?" Louisa asked. Better to humor her mother, especially since Louisa had to admit some pretty strange things happened at the old homestead since her father had died. She wasn't at all sure her mother didn't "see" Rob Garrett. "Why don't I make us a nice cup of tea and you can tell me all about your day?"

"That would be grand," Hattie replied. "By the way, your da said to tell you the baby is a girl."

"That's nice, Ma." She put the few things she had carried in from the barn in the corner of the living room and went to start the fire in the belly of the old wood stove. She then sat next to her mother on the sofa as Hattie regaled her with what her father had to say about the baby.

She awoke to the distant whistling of a teakettle. For a moment she was disoriented. Where was Ma and why did the cabin seem so different? Then she realized that she was in Lee's home and his bed. In a moment, he entered after a soft knock. "I made us some tea. How are you feeling?"

"Other than being a bit sore and stiff, a lot better."

Lee pulled a chair next to the bed. He sat and handed her a steaming cup. She took a sip. It tasted different than any tea she was used to, yet it was vaguely familiar. "What is this. It's different. Somehow I think I have tasted it before but I can't place it."

"Sassafras tea. Some of the local people dig the bushes and make a tea from the bark. Like it?"

"Yes. Somehow it reminds me of drinking old fashioned root beer when I was a kid."

"Your granny probably made it and may have given you some as a child. It's considered a medicine around here. It's supposed to be a diuretic and a general tonic. I'm no doctor but since you have a lot of swelling in your ankle, it couldn't hurt."

They sipped the tea in a companionable silence

for a while. "Where are the puppies? I thought you let them inside sometimes."

"I do, sometimes, but their manners still leave a lot to be desired. I banished them to the yard so you could sleep without a couple of Hounds from Hell tromping all over you in bed." His smile let her know he had long ago forgiven her remarks about his dogs. "By the way, I would never have pegged Velma Lou for the domestic type but she called while you were sleeping and offered to straighten up your cabin so you wouldn't have to face that mess again. I offered to come down and give her a hand but she insisted she could handle it.' He shrugged.

"Well. I guess there is a heart of gold under Velma Lou's brash exterior."

He produced a small packet of papers from his back pocket. "We never did get around to looking at these old papers the workmen found in my kitchen wall. Feel up to it?"

"Great, I want to tell you about the things I learned when I was…what do I call it? Time traveling? Whatever this is that I'm doing. It has to be the diary and the quilt. I tried when I first laid down without the quilt. It didn't work until I got the quilt and covered with it. Then I was there in a flash." She could see Lee was going to comment. "No, don't say anything unless you can give me any other explanation. Could we go down to the den and sit? I feel like an invalid or a sex pot sitting in bed in the middle of the day."

He leered, "Humm, now that gives me some ideas. Sex pot, you say?"

She laughed. "That does it. We definitely need to get downstairs so I can get your mind focusing on the right things."

He stared at the tee shirt pulled tight over her breasts and watched her nipples harden. "I'd say I was focusing on some pretty interesting things right now."

"Later, sex maniac. This is important."

He helped her out of bed and handed her the cane. "I could carry you downstairs," he offered "but if you want to talk, you had better at least put on a pair of shorts under that shirt. I'm having a definite problem concentrating, at least on the past."

He made her comfortable on the leather sofa and pulled a little round walnut table over next to it.

"One thing we could do," he began "is check dates. Do you know from family history or anything, the dates of the things you are 'witnessing' as your granny?"

"I suppose some of them might have been something I was told, but my mother wasn't big on family history so I doubt if I was told everything I now know. And Lillith's baby, Anne, I didn't know anything about her. She would have been Velma Lou's great grandmother. I could always ask her, but I think we ought to look at the papers you found first. Maybe there is something there."

The papers were brittle and stiff. The handwriting was rounded and slanted, the style of another era. The first papers had no significance to Louisa's diary. They were military records that related to Donald Stuart's service in the Confederate Army. Then they found an envelope addressed to Louisa Garrett from Donald Stuart. It had the phrase "Do not open until my death" written in block letters under the name. With trembling hands, Casey opened it and unfolded the fragile paper. It was dated May 1st, 1879. She began to read. *My dearest Louisa, There are thing I need to tell you but I don't rightly know if I should. I will be betrayin a promise, revealin a secret I should take to my grave. But I knowed I had to confide in you about the whereabouts of the treasure. It'll place a heavy burden on you should anyone, specially*

Lillith, discover that you know. I decided you are the only person I can trust. I'll tell you a shocking secret but you must not reveal it to anyone. As to the treasure, I'll give you a map you are not to open unless you are in dire straits financially. Even then, think twice. This money has cost the lives of too many people already. It should only be used to repair the damage done by the terrible war that spawned it in the first place.

But first, let me tell you the tale that has burdened my heart for thirteen years.

You are my daughter. As you know, I love Lillith. I have since she was a tiny girl in pigtails who even then caused a riff between David and myself. We were two years older than she was. I can still see her strollin up the path to the cabin we lived in then. David didn't want her to tag along as we did all of the "boy" things like fishin and whittlin. I could not turn her away even then. She grew more beautiful as she approached womanhood. Alas, she knew the power of her beauty and used it well. When I returned from the war on leave that last time in the winter of '65, I knew I would do anything to make her my wife. She wanted to leave the mountains even then. I promised her I'd take her away after the war. She promised to marry me when I returned. She was just 14 then but already she was experienced in the ways of men and women. We made love in the woods and the barn. Anyplace we could find to be alone. When I left at the end of March, I didn't know she was in a family way.

When I returned in May, with the treasury gold, I told her I couldn't leave the mountains. I tried to explain why but to her the treasure was all the more reason to leave. I still didn't know she was carrying my child, you. Perhaps if I had.... but I only found out after you were born. She never came near me for months. I tried to forget her. I was busy buildin the new house. Trying to make my mother's last days more comfortable. The first time I realized was when I heard Hatty had had a baby. I had seen her one day when I walked down to talk to Rob. She stepped out for just a minute then ducked back. I thought nothin of it at the time. It was only later I realized you were Lillith's child. My child. The timing was right. There was no question in my mind. Lillith finally admitted it to me but made me understand that I would only be hurtin Rob and Hattie. She still wouldn't marry me so there was no point. She told me she would one day find a man who would take her away to a big city no matter what she had to do.

Remember when I told you a few weeks ago that it wasn't Lillith that shot the preacher, I know who did. I am not sure what I am going to do about it but it's been on my conscience. I need to deal with that soon. Lillith had been seein the preacher. Trying to get him to leave his wife and run away with her. David had been seein her too. He begged me to tell him where the treasure is hidden. I can't. You see, I know he has been in love with Lillith for a long time. He would take it and use it to take her wherever she wants to go. He's not a strong person, but he's my brother. My kith and kin. He's afraid to go with out any money but he is desperate to get Lillith. When I wouldn't tell him where the gold is he was afraid the preacher would win her- I can't say love since I know she is incapable of love- but her body. I know you are too young to understand this now but later you will understand. I know I will go to my grave lovin Lillith yet I know what she can do to a man. I understand why David felt he had to kill the preacher. I am going to confront David and give him some money so he can go away but not with her. Never with Lillith. I have to tell the sheriff what I know but I don't want to be the one who puts my own brother behind bars.

Dear Little One, I am wanderin. I want you to understand all the misery the treasure has caused. If I had never taken it, I would have married Lillith and left here. Perhaps we would all be a happy family in Atlanta. Jonathan would still be alive. My brother would not be a murderer. I have buried the treasure in the last place anyone will ever look for it. I have already put the map in the cabin. It is in granny's hole. Leave it there unless you can put it to a use that justifies all the lives it cost. I hear David comin. I will hide this for now and finish it later. I must talk to him. I cannot keep silent any longer.

With tears in her eyes, Casey looked up from the unfinished letter. "Louisa never knew. David must have killed him before he could finish it."

"So there really was a treasure after all. Your granny wasn't just telling you tall tales."

"Yes. Even though she never got the letter, she was always suspicious of David. She must have wanted to tell someone before she died and I was the only one even though I was too young to understand."

"Do you know what he means when he says the map's in the cabin, then it's in 'granny's hole'."

"No. Maybe it's buried with one of his grandmothers but I don't know who they were or where they are buried."

Lee thought a moment. "Maybe he was hurrying to hide the letter from David and didn't realize what he was writing. Maybe he would have cleared it up when he finished the letter."

"Maybe but we'll never know. I'm not sure I really want that treasure considering all the bad luck it brought."

Just then, the phone rang. Lee spoke for a few minutes then returned to the couch. "Well, that was my Great Aunt Mary. I had called her about the preacher's son being adopted. She knows more of the family's history that any one. She returned my call and confirmed that a couple named Hiram and Joanne Schmidt adopted my great grandfather's father in 1880. All the family records have about this was that his name was Andrew Jonathan. No surname but she said there were stories when she was a girl about the fact that his natural father was a preacher who died involved in some kind of scandal. It fits too closely to be a coincidence."

"I don't believe in coincidences," Casey stated. "Like, what are the odds that my house would be broken into twice in one month? Especially in a low crime area like this. Something is going on that I don't understand. Think about it, Lee, what is at the heart of all these coincidences?" She paused for a minute to see if he was on the same wavelength.

"The diary." He confirmed her thought.

"Right. It's been the catalyst in this entire affair. Why did all of these things start happening after I found it? Why does some force, for want of a more spectacular word like ghost, seem to be hiding the diary from whoever wants it? And the biggest question, who could possibly want it that bad?"

They finally agreed that the diary had no monetary value to anyone other than as a historic document. Lee wanted her to stay at his house until everything was settled but Casey was not sure if that was what she wanted. She felt so helpless not only because she had to hobble around with the help of Lee or the cane when he went to work. Lee took good care of her needs, cooking fetching whatever she needed. He gently carried her up and down the stairs so she wouldn't feel so confined. He offered to bring Smokey up to keep her company, but each time he did the old tom returned as if it was his self-appointed job to tend the cabin. He had never forgiven Tater and Snuffy for chasing him, even though they accepted him now. In fact they wanted to play. Smokey just hissed, puffed his back up and showed his claws. The pups decided to find another playmate. Casey grew to love them, too. They really were just mischievous babies in spite of their size. Lee checked on Smokey's food and water daily. At first, Lee insisted he would sleep on the sofa so as not to bother her ankle. Casey finally convinced him that her ankle really had nothing to do with her sex life. After that, they made gentle love every night and often in the morning or afternoons when Lee came home early from work. He had finally purchased condoms and insisted on using them.

True to her word, Velma Lou had cleaned the cabin and repeated her offer to Casey to stay at her house if she preferred. By the end of the next week, Casey's ankle was back to normal and she was chafing at the bit to get back to work. Besides, the longer she stayed here at Lee's house, the more natural it seemed. She was afraid her feelings were getting out of control. She needed a little space to sort out her emotions; the memories of the disastrous marriage to Ray were too fresh in her mind.

On Friday, she decided to surprise Lee with a special meal since he had either cooked or brought take out home since she had been injured. She decided on an old fashioned meatloaf, mashed potatoes and mixed vegetables. For dessert, she found Lee had a carton of hand dipped French vanilla ice cream in his freezer. She had recently bought a flat of raspberries and, since she couldn't eat all of them before they went bad, had frozen some. She decided to mix up the meatloaf, boil the Yukon Gold Potatoes and then go to her cabin for the raspberries. She set the oven on 300 degrees and turned the potatoes down to simmer. Satisfied that they would be safe for a quick trip to the cabin, she set off down the path. Tater and Snuffy followed her to the cabin, then returned home.

Inside, Smokey greeted her on the porch with his usual ankle twining and plaintive meows. She spent several minutes scratching under his chin to the accompaniment of his loud purr of approval. Inside, everything was spotless. Velma Lou had done a terrific job. That reminded her she needed to call her cousin and let her know she was raring to get back to work.

There was no answer at her house or the office but Velma Lou picked up on the first ring when Casey tried her cell phone. "Funny, I was just thinking about you."

"I am at the cabin and it looks lovely. I really do appreciate it, Velma Lou." Casey continued, "I need to get back to work. How about Monday?"

"Actually," her cousin replied, "There is a little something you can do for me now. If you're up to it, of course. I have a piece one of the high school girls did and I need someone to proof it and maybe puff it up a bit. I could bring it by the cabin. I'm just a few minutes away."

"Okay, if you can be here in less than 10 minutes, I left something on the fire at Lee's house. Or you could give me a few minutes and come by there."

"No. Wait at the cabin. I'll swing by there. I don't want to interfere with you two love birds. He's not there with you, is he?"

"No. He's not home yet. I'm cooking a special dinner for him."

After talking to Velma Lou, Casey wandered around her cabin. She touched the old headboard that some unknown craftsman had made by hand. The clothes press that had once held Granny's things was more precious than any new chest of drawers from a store. She spoke out loud to the presence she always sensed in the cabin. "Granny, are you somehow here?" No answer, of course. What had she expected? Her granny to speak from the grave? Then, all the lights flickered and then went out. One by one, the ceiling fixtures she had gotten installed years ago in an effort to entice Ray to visit the mountains with her, swayed. As she watched, the swaying became more frantic until, one by one, all of the fixtures fell to the floor. The bulbs broke and scattered. The exposed wires flickered ominously. Smokey looked imploringly at her and scampered through his cat door. Casey decided, for once, she was going to follow the scary cat's example and get out. She needed to get back to Lee's house and call the fire department before everything went up in flames.

She rushed out and made it to the foot of the stairs. Suddenly, she was engulfed in a foul smelling cloth. It kept her from seeing the person who held it over her head, but she could feel the gun he was holding to her side. The last thing she glimpsed was Smokey racing away from the cabin at breakneck speed. The crazy thought rushed through her head, *fine friend you are to desert me now.* How silly. What help could one chicken hearted cat be against an armed gunman?

"One move, bitch, and I'll blow your head off and stuff you in the septic tank, too."

Petrified, Casey couldn't have moved if she tried. He secured the blanket over her head, shoulders and upper arms with a tightly fastened belt around her waist. She quivered, "What do you want?"

"Where is the dammed book?"

"The book?"

"Don't play dumb with me, you stupid bitch. I want that dairy."

"It's not on me. I'll have to go get it. You can have it." Casey's mind was racing. If she could stall her assailant, Velma Lou would be along shortly and perhaps that would scare him off.

"I know it's not in the cabin. For the last time," he pushed the gun more firmly into her side to emphasize his point, "where is it?"

"The house up on the hill." She sensed, rather than saw, her captor glance uphill.

"Oh, shit! Somebody's coming down the path." He grabbed her and half dragged, half led her to her car. She could feel him open the door on the passenger side. "Unless you want your boyfriend's brains scattered all over your yard, don't say anything."

Casey knew without seeing what was happening. She dared not try to warn Lee. The silence stretched interminably. If only she knew what was happening. The blanket was held firmly in place and she dared not squirm to try and work it off when she didn't know if the gunman was watching her. She could hear Lee's footsteps approaching. He called "Casey? Casey, are you here?"

How she longed to warn him away but she didn't dare make a sound. She heard a rustle next to her just outside the car. The grip on her arm slackened.

"That's far enough, Sir Galahad. I've got the fair maiden trussed up like a turkey and if you make one false move, her goose is cooked."

She heard Lee's "Okay. Okay. I'll do whatever you want. Just don't hurt her."

"Smart boy. Turn around and back up to the passenger side of her car, then put your hands behind your back so I can tie them."

"What are you going to do to us? If it's money you want, my wallet is back at the house but I'll be glad to give you whatever you want." Lee spoke in a careful, soft voice. She could tell he was not going to lose his head and try any thing foolish.

"I want that dammed book but I'll have to take care of you two before I go up to your house and get it."

"Take care of us? What are you going to do? I told you, you can have the dairy. It's just an old book. It's not worth anything." Casey asked.

"It's a little too late for that. You two might be able to identify me," the assailant growled.

"How could we?" Lee reasoned. "You have that bandana over your face and she's all covered with that blanket. Why add murder to your crimes? You'll never get away with it."

"Yes, I will. Now quit stalling and start backing up over here." Over the menacing voice, Casey heard a ferocious barking, hissing and spitting. A yelp of canine pain pierced the night. She heard the thunder of paws racing down the path towards them. The intruder heard the disturbance at the same moment. He loosened his grasp on Casey's arm. Immediately she struggled free from the throng holding the smelly blanket in place and was greeted with the sight of the barking dogs inches behind a hissing fluffed up Smokey. At the last moment, Smokey veered directly into the masked man, throwing him off balance momentarily as he sought to escape what appeared to be two ferocious hounds intent on tearing anything in their way into shreds. The split second interruption was enough for Lee. He swung into action. Casey had never seen any human move so fast. He had their attacker pinned to the ground and yanked off the bandanna in one fluid move.

"Mayor Campbell!" Casey exclaimed in astonishment.

"Why?" Lee demanded as he yanked the fallen man's arm a bit higher.

"You're breaking my arm!" Then the pups, who had lost all interest in Smokey, perched high in the nearest dogwood tree, nosed him and Lee, thinking this was a new game. "Keep those monsters away from me. They're vicious."

"They're not, but I may be if you don't tell me what's going on." Lee demanded.

"I want my lawyer. Before I say anything."

Lee dropped the man's arm in disgust. "Hand me that rope he had around you so I can tie him up."

Casey passed over the rope and gingerly accepted the gun Lee pressed into her hand. "Hold this on him while I secure his hands." He expertly tied the mayor's hands, and for good measure, looped the rope over his feet as well. He turned to Casey. "You hold that gun on him while I go call the sheriff. If he makes one move, shoot to kill."

"I can't shoot," Casey quavered.

"Yes, you can," Lee calmly declared. "It's easier than having you go back up those stairs with your bad ankle." He indicated the trigger. "The safety is off. All you need to do is press this if he even breathes hard."

"Don't do this," the fallen man pleaded. "She will probably shoot me accidentally. I won't try anything. I just want my lawyer."

"No great loss if she does," Lee countered. "I'll swear she shot you as you tried to escape." He turned and rushed up the stairs.

Remembering the fallen light fixtures, Casey called after him, "Be careful, all the lights are down. Call the fire department too."

As she waited, Smokey came down from the tree and proceeded to rub around her ankles, totally ignoring the pups now sleeping near her feet. "I believe the three of you staged that fight just to save our lives," Casey murmured.

Smokey just purred harder and looked at his human with round yellow eyes. The pups snored gently.

Lee gingerly pushed open the cabin door. From Casey's statement, he expected it to be in shambles, maybe already beginning an electrical fire. Instead the cabin appeared in perfect order. The lights hung in their usual place on the ceiling. When he tried the switch, they came on. Shrugging his shoulders, he picked up the phone and called Sheriff Cole. As he headed back out the door, he took in the strange scene below. The sight of the woman he loved stroking the purring cat stirred his soul. His rambunctious pups slept nearby. Something was strange. He would have sworn that cat was no more afraid of the pups than he was. Yet their actions had saved his life. Could Casey be right about something mystical in her cabin? He knew her well enough to know if she said she saw the light fixtures crash to the ground, she had not imagined it. His scientist mind for a minute accepted things outside the realm of science. Like benevolent spirits. Like traveling back in time. Like love. Yes, love. That was surely outside the realm of reason. Why would a sane person seek the very thing that has hurt so deeply in the past? Yet, he now accepted that he was in love with Casey. When he saw that man holding a gun on her, it all came together. He would gladly have laid down his own life to protect her. That had to be love. There was new tenderness in his touch when he took the gun from her hand and put the other arm around her trembling shoulders. "You can cry now if you need to. The sheriff is on his way."

"Thank God." She slumped against him. "What about the fire department? Is there any sign of a fire where those wires broke?"

He shook his head. "You're not going to believe this but there is nothing wrong with the lights in the cabin. I think something was trying to warn you to get out of there."

"Something?" she queried.

"Alright." He shrugged. "I'm becoming a believer in your supernatural phenomena. If I can accept time travel via an old diary, I guess a friendly ghost is not too hard to accept."

The sheriff arrived and had Dirk Campbell in the back of his patrol car in just seconds. If he felt any surprise at their story, he hid it well. Even the fallen lights that were back in place didn't faze him. "We'll let him call his lawyer from the station and then let you know what we find out." He looked at the peaceful array of animals nearby. "Sure is lucky those dogs decided to chase the cat at just the right time. They don't look like they are interested in it all now." The sheriff rubbed his head and then looked up the path in alarm. "Oh, oh! Looks like you do need the fire department after all." Spirals of black smoked drifted up in the direction of Lee's house.

"Oh, my God! The meatloaf!" Casey exclaimed. The sheriff was already on the police radio alerting the fire department.

It was almost an hour later when the fire chief

gave them the all clear. The kitchen was in shambles, more damage caused by the water and smoke than the fire. Lee surveyed the damage. It was disheartening but not devastating. He had insurance and it would take a few weeks to repair the damage but it could be put back as good as before. The same could not be said for Casey's dairy. He saw her slumped in a chair on the porch holding the charred dripping book in her lap. The tears flowed down her cheeks unimpaired. His heart went out to her. He wondered if she had any idea how lovely she looked to him at that moment. Mussed hair, smudged makeup, clothes in disarray and ripped from her struggles to escape from beneath the blanket used to imprison her; still, to him, she was lovely. He touched her hand. "I'm so sorry about your granny's dairy," he murmured.

"Oh, Lee, I'm so selfish sitting here wallowing in sorrow over a silly book while your whole kitchen and half of your beautiful home is destroyed. It's all my fault. I completely forgot the meatloaf when Campbell grabbed me."

"It'd not your fault. You've been through too much for any one person to stand." He looked down at her and realized how much worse he would feel if he had not left without a thought of the stove when he found her gone. "You could have been killed. I can replace the house even if it had been totally destroyed. But you," he enveloped her in his arms, "I never want to be without you."

"All I could think of when I heard you coming down the path was that he would kill you and I would never get to tell you how much I love you." She burst into a fresh batch of tears.

He cuddled her close. She wasn't attempting to be one bit seductive but he could feel his fly straining. "If we don't stop this, I'm going to end up making love to you right here on this wet dirty floor. Let me grab a few things and we'll go to your place where we can get your ankle propped up in a clean bed. That is if you don't mind putting me up for a few days until I can get this repaired?"

She gazed up at him. "You can stay in my cabin for as long as you like. However, I have a better use for the bed than propping up my ankle," she grinned mischievously.

"Well that's an invitation guaranteed to make me get my things packed in record time. You just wait here. I'll be back down in a minute."

It was many minutes later when they lay together in the old oak bed, both thoroughly depleted by their mutually satisfying lovemaking. Lee gazed adoringly down into Casey's eyes. "How do you feel about marriage?"

She sat up abruptly. "Marriage?"

"Yeah. You know that 'for better or worse' thing?"

"I have to give that some thought. Right now, do you know what I want?"

"Anything you want, I'll try to give you." Even as he said it, he felt corny; but it really was how he felt about Casey.

She popped out of bed with little care for her sore ankle. "Good, you can buy me a pizza."

"A pizza? I thought you would ask for jewelry or something big."

"All right. Make it a big pizza. A big pepperoni pizza."

He laughed. "Your wish is my command. But if Nancy is closed, we may have to drive all the way to Atlanta."

Nancy wasn't closed when they arrived. She was sitting at a booth checking the day's receipts with Miz Maggie. She promised that if they waited for her oven to reheat, she would make them the biggest pizza they had ever had. They just had to wait to tell the story of the day's happenings until she had it in the oven. "Granny can entertain you while I put it together then we can all get fat on the gooey cheese and heaping helpings of pepperoni I plan to put on it."

When Nancy rejoined them, Casey told the story of their eventful day with a few interruptions from Lee. Afterwards, they began speculation on why Dirk Campbell would want the diary bad enough to kill for it. "I never voted for him no how," Miz Maggie concluded. "There was always something a little slippery about him. Just goes to show how bad Velma Lou's taste in men is. She had him sniffin' around after her."

"Velma Lou!" Casey exclaimed. "She was supposed to bring over some papers for me to work on. She must have tried to call and thought I left. I've got to call her. Can I use the phone?"

She returned to the table a few minutes later. "I couldn't reach her. She isn't answering any of the numbers. Not even her cell phone. She must have given up on me. I hope nothing happened to her."

Miz Maggie snorted, "That un's too mean for anything to happen to. She probably met some good lookin' fella and forgot all about you. I wouldn't worry none."

Over coffee, they told Maggie and Nancy about the strange entry in the diary. Maggie laughed so hard the tears streamed down her face. "Lordy. I know you both ain't from around here but any old mountain folk could tell you what 'Granny's hole' is. You got a small round window in yer cabin near the fireplace, don't cha?"

"Yes," Casey replied.

"Well, that's it." She looked from one to the other. Lee wondered how he could feel so stupid with all his degrees next to this uneducated mountain woman who knew so many things that were not taught in any college.

She continued, "In the old days in the mountains, everybody had to pull their weight. You did what you could to help. The old granny in the family, who couldn't do too much else, could sit next to this window and keep an eye on the fire and watch for anybody approaching and let the family know who was coming. Thus it was called 'Granny's hole'."

They thanked her and made ready to leave. Nancy wouldn't take any payment for the pizza. "It was on the house."

It was then that Miz Maggie looked from one to the other. "I guess congratulation are in order."

Lee couldn't hide the surprise. "I just asked her tonight. How did you know?"

Casey seemed equally surprised. "I haven't said yes yet."

Miz Maggie chuckled. "You ain't got no say in this. That little baby gal will be arrivin' in about eight months. I recon' you had better consider making a good home for her."

Back at Casey's cabin, they tried to assimilate the news Miz Maggie had so abruptly dumped in their laps. The idea of a baby was too emotionally charged in both their minds to deal with just jet.

Instead, by unspoken mutual consent, they concentrated on the idea of the map's hiding place. The small round window commanded their interest. It was well made. The white oak plank had been skillfully turned to create the inside framing of the tiny round window. It was made in three separate pieces. On close inspection, each piece had several grooves cut into the upper face of the plank. The deep grooves carefully spaced at regular intervals no longer showed unless the wood was inspected closely. The grooves, combined with judicious soaking of the plank, had allowed the early carpenter, Rob Garrett, to create a tight fitting frame. Gently, they pried up the bottom section of the windowsill. Casey couldn't bear the thought of breaking this piece of the cabin that had been so lovingly constructed by Louisa's father, so they pried with a small crow bar just a fraction of an inch at a time. The ancient wood frame had sat in this very spot for so long it seemed reluctant to be parted from its base. After what seemed like hours, but was in fact only about fifteen minutes, the wood gave up the struggle and popped easily out of place.

Lee and Casey strained to peer down into the dark opening it revealed. "Can't see a thing," Casey murmured.

"I'll get a flashlight," Lee stated. With the strong beam aimed down into the hole, they were able to see an unusual object setting near floor level within the wall. They pulled the bundle out and brushed off the cobwebs accumulated over its century and a quarter rest. Sure enough, there was a roll of fragile paper wrapped in an oiled cloth. They gently unrolled it and spread it on the table. It was a simple map that showed several landmarks, some that were no longer in existence but enough that were to be able to decipher its secret. Both the cabin and the Stuart place were identified. It clearly showed the treasure chest buried directly under the floor of what had been the old barn, now the thickest part of the Kudzu growth that covered the patch of land where the barn had once stood.

"It's somewhere near the property line that divide these two places today," Lee murmured in surprise. "If it's what you want, tomorrow we can call someone with a bobcat to start digging."

"Yes," Casey replied. "It might have brought disaster to those who had it in the past, but it's time it started doing some good. I have a few ideas how it can be used to help the local people and still preserve the memory of Donald Stuart and all he stood for."

When the map was put carefully into a drawer and they sat facing each other over a cup of steaming tea, they both recognized the time was right to consider facing the even more important news about a child. Lee was still a little skeptical about a baby but

Casey felt that she was, in fact, pregnant. A lot of small changes in her body proclaimed the truth in Miz Maggie's words. The way she had felt nauseous a few times in the past week. At the time, she had attributed it to the sprained ankle and the excitement. But it fit. It did fit. In her heart, she knew she wanted this child and would have it no matter how Lee felt about it.

The smile on Lee's face told her he was probably just as thrilled with the news once he began to assimilate it. He chuckled, "It's a good thing I asked you to marry me before we found this out or you would just think I was trying to 'make an honest woman' out of you."

Casey thought about his comment for a moment before she answered. "I know I do love you, but I am still frightened about the idea of marriage. Ray seemed 'Mr. Wonderful' while we were dating but…"

"I am not Ray," Lee interrupted. "I love you and would never do anything to put you down. Can't you see all men are not like that? He probably had such a self esteem problem that he had to put others down to try to make himself feel adequate. You were an easy target."

"I know. Logically I know. Let's just sleep on it. I'm exhausted and not in shape to think right now after all that's happened.

Long after Lee's breathing told her he was sound asleep, Casey lay awake. The loss of the dairy on top of everything else left her feeling adrift. Maybe a cup of tea would help her sleep. She gently disengaged the arm and leg Lee had wrapped around her. In the kitchen, she boiled the water and seeped the Chamomile Tea for a few minutes. The steam drifted upward and through it, she seemed to see Granny Weesie sitting across the room in her old rocker. "You're not really here," Casey murmured more to herself than in acknowledgement of the presence.

"Yes, I am, Child. I have been here watching over you all these years. But it's time for me to go. I need to move on. You're ready to face things on you own now. O' course with that fine young man, you're not on your own exactly." The apparition smiled and Casey felt an overwhelming happiness and a small sadness at the same time.

"Oh, Granny, I have felt you here so many times. That is why I had to come back when I was hurting so badly after Ray and I divorced. The cabin will seem so empty without your presence."

"'To all things there is a season.' My season is past. It's your time now. Yours and that young'un. She's the part o' me that goes on. An' a part of Donald and Daniel and Jonathan and even a part o' Lillith. Things have come full circle at last. I know what you are planning with the money and it's a good thing. Love your young man. I never got the chance with Jonathan. Maybe that was not a real love anyway, just a girlish heart's first flutterin'. I knew a different kind of happiness with Daniel. We had something that was real. It just took me a long time to understand that love has different faces sometimes. It's only because of all those things that happened in my life that you are here today. Life is short, Child, use yours well. Don't waste it." The shadowy image gradually faded.

"Oh, Granny, I'll always remember you," Casey sobbed. And she thought she heard the echo of an answer in the wind that moaned outside the cabin.

"Life is for the living."

The next day dawned bright and clear. Casey awoke feeling at one with the weather. She gently kissed Lee awake. "I want to give you an answer to that question. It's yes. Yes. Yes!"

Lee was now fully aroused in more ways than one. He enveloped her in a crushing hug. "You'll never regret it, Casey. I love you so much. I was so afraid you would be scared to take another chance on marriage. I won't even ask what made you decide."

"I had a long talk with Granny last night. She convinced me it was time to bury the dead. That included dead marriages. It's time to move on." She began to cuddle closer to his warm body.

"I totally agree with Granny's ghost, even if I am not sure I totally believe in her. Speaking of 'moving on', if you move your hand just a little lower, you'll see just how much you move me."

She did and it was much later before they were ready to get out of bed.

In fact, if the phone hadn't startled them out of their preoccupation with one another, they would have spent the rest of the day naked under the old patchwork quilt.

It was a bewildered Sheriff Cole. "I need you to come down to the station. I made another rather surprising arrest in your assault case."

Lee had to take care of some work at the Experiment Station so Casey drove downtown to the police station. Sheriff Cole led her into a small gray room. "Last night, Dirk wouldn't say a word until he got his lawyer here. It wasn't until this morning, that the lawyer, Marty Cleveland, got here that he would tell us anything. Then he offered us a bargain. He'd plead out and give us the person behind the scheme in exchange for a ten-year sentence. He promised to clear up the Zeke case, too, if he had immunity. Since the motive was shaky and he had no priors, the DA accepted and you'll never guess who he named." The sheriff stopped as if waiting for a guess.

"No, I couldn't guess. Why not tell me," Casey replied.

"Your cousin, Velma Lou. That's who. He said he would talk to us more after we questioned her and understood things better."

"Velma Lou? But why?" Casey remembered her cousin's attempts to gain access to the diary. It was beginning to make a murky kind of sense.

"That's why we called you. She says she is ready to confess but wants to do it directly to you." The sheriff wiped his forehead with a non-too-clean bandanna. "So if you're willing, we'll bring her in along with a court reporter to take down her statement. Are you up to facing her?"

Casey nodded. "I think I am beginning to understand."

"Well, you're way ahead of me. All I got so far is something about an old book." He shook his head. "I can't figure any old book being important enough to kill two people for."

A few minutes later, Velma Lou was led into the

small interrogation room. Her usually shining hair was matted. She wore no makeup and was clad in the orange jail jumpsuit. If Casey didn't know she was confronting her cousin, she would not have believed this haggard middle aged looking woman was Velma Lou. She did not look Casey in the eye. She fumbled with a glass of water on the table in front of her. Finally, when everyone indicated they were ready, she spoke in a low but audible voice. "Casey, darlin', I'm sorry for trying to kill you. I never really meant to hurt you but it all just escalated. You see, I wanted the diary. I knew about the treasure for a while. It had been rumored and scraps of information passed down in the family. I'm not getting any younger and I wanted to move up. This town was stifling me. I had achieved all I could accomplish here. I needed a bigger pond to fish in. I needed a lot of money to buy a major paper in one of the bigger cities. The treasure seemed like my only chance. I tried to get you to give it to me without hurting you. I tried to get you to go out of town and sell me the cabin. I guess I became obsessed with the treasure. But can't you understand? It was my only way out. Without it, I couldn't move up." She finally looked at Casey directly. "I know you can't forgive me but I want you to know, I never really wanted to kill you. You just put us in a spot where there was no choice." The pleading look in her eyes turned hard again. "Dirk messed it all up. I knew I never should have trusted a man to do the job. They all let you down in the end." She began sobbing.

The deputies led the broken woman back to her cell. "Do you know what she meant?" Sheriff Cole asked.

Briefly, Casey explained about their mutual family background. She told of finding the old diary. "I think I know why she wanted it so badly. What's going to happen to her now?"

"Well, since she's pleading guilty, there won't be a trial. She sounded pretty unstable to me. She may go to prison for a few years or she may be committed to a mental institute."

"It's so sad," Casey commented. "If she had only been satisfied with what she had achieved here in Bluejay. She built that paper up from almost nothing."

"Some folks are never satisfied. It's a case of 'The grass is always greener..'," the sheriff replied. "Incidentally, we have a full confession from Dirk Campbell, too." He studied a sheaf of papers a deputy had thrust into his hand as he sat talking to Casey. "He claims Velma Lou killed Zeke and he only helped her after the fact by stashing him in your septic tank. He said that Zeke finally figured that if it wasn't him harassing you, it had to be someone else. Velma Lou had paid his cousin to tamper with the brakes the first time. Cousin Laz decided to get out of town but before he left, he told Zeke. Zeke decided that was too good a blackmail possibility to pass up. Velma Lou paid him as long as it was useful to have him as a suspect but when he got arrested the last time, he told her if he got picked up again he would snitch on her. He knew of her involvement with Campbell and figured she could pull strings. Campbell knew there was no point in even trying to interfere with me doing my job, so he told Velma Lou she had to deal with Zeke the best way she could. Could be the truth since the bullet in Zeke's head seems to match Velma Lou's gun. We haven't gotten the ballistics test back yet, but I have a hunch it will just confirm that it was the gun used to kill Zeke Folsome. Campbell said that he and Velma Lou were going to make it look like you had killed Zeke. You weren't going to be around to dispute her statement. You, and Lee after he got involved, were going to be put in your car and pushed over the steepest part of Insurance Point. Velma Lou was going to say she sent you on some assignment up that way and you must have lost control of your car and driven off the side of the mountain. Campbell was going to loosen the brakes again and that way it would look like Tom hadn't fixed it right or maybe there was something that made the brake line work loose. Says it was all to get the old diary you mentioned. Any idea why it was so important to her?"

"She thinks it will lead her to a buried treasure. Since it originally belonged, sort of, to my great grandmother's father, it would belong to me if anyone actually finds it. Of course, if I were dead, Velma Lou is my nearest living relative."

"All this is over a treasure? Is it real?"

"Oh yes, sheriff, I believe it's very real. I guess Velma Lou believed it too or she wouldn't have been willing to kill me for it. Anyway, we'll know for sure this afternoon. Lee was going to arrange with someone who worked on his house to get a bobcat in there and dig it up. Would you like to join us? If you follow me back to the cabin, they may have the equipment set to dig by now."

Sheriff Cole was more than anxious to see what had precipitated the unexpected crime wave in his little community. When they pulled into Casey's driveway, they found Lee and the bobcat owner, Max, ready to go. They had already cleared the area of much of the growth of Kudzu and had located the remains of some posts in the ground that probably were the old barn's corner posts. "We were just waiting for you, Casey," Lee stated. He gave the signal to the waiting operator and the digging began in earnest.

Max sank the blade into the ground slowly and deposited the yard or so of earth on the side of the clearing. After about eight shovel's full, the blade struck something more solid than red clay. It didn't sound like a rock would. Lee signaled Max to cut the machine off and he began probing with a small shovel. Max jumped down and began to clear the other side; and in minutes, they had unearthed a black metal box about twenty by sixteen inches and about a ten inches high. The two men brushed off as much of the dirt that clung to the box as they could, then Lee handed it to Casey. "You deserve to open this. It is rightfully yours."

Casey touched the pitted side of the box. It was so little and unprepossessing to hold so much history, let alone whatever amount of money it contained. She was almost afraid to open it. Perhaps like Pandora, she would let loose a whole new set of troubles. No more negative thinking, she chided herself. She pulled the top open. It was stiff and old, and creaked and groaned before popping open to reveal its secrets. The contents were enclosed in a faded white cotton drawstring bag. With trembling fingers, Casey lifted the bag. It was heavy. The material was disintegrating in her hand. Reverently, she pushed the cloth aside. The warm glint of four solid gold blocks were exposed to the light of day for the first time in over a hundred and twenty years. "It's beautiful," she exclaimed. Tears streamed down her cheeks at the thought of all that was represented by the gold bricks.

The men all started to speak at one time. "Hot damn!" Max exhaled.

"It's worth a fortune!" Sheriff Cole commented.

"It's your chance to make your dreams come true, Casey," Lee whispered.

"No. It's going to make Donald Stuart's dream come true. He lost his life because he refused to use this for his selfish purpose. It came out of a horrible war that split our nation. It is destined to be used for good, not evil."

Sheriff Cole queried, "Used for good? Care to

explain what you have in mind?"

Casey touched the worn chest and looked up the hill at Lee's "Old Stuart House", now almost finished its second renovation. The swarm of carpenters had returned the kitchen to the state it had been in before the fire. She and Lee had discussed moving back into it tomorrow. She looked down at her own small cabin. She would miss it, but what she had in mind was what the cabin deserved; what Granny Weesie would have wanted. "I'm going to hold a press conference tomorrow at noon to explain what I have in mind. Any chance of holding it at the sheriff's office since it concerns this community?"

"I'd be honored since I seem to have been caught up in this thing since the beginning," the sheriff replied as he headed for his car.

Casey and Lee arrived at the Sheriff's office a little before noon. They had already made two stops. One at the courthouse to apply for a marriage license, then to Nancy's where Casey and Miz Maggie huddled over a large pepperoni pizza while Lee and Nancy discussed the best appliances for a small food service operation.

Promptly at twelve, Casey stepped out front and addressed the small group of media people drawn by the rumors of a story of hidden gold and old scandals. She told the story of the hidden treasure and the family history that went with it in a straightforward manner. She didn't touch on Velma Lou and Dirk Campbell's arrest at all, in spite of clamors by the reporters for answers. Instead, she referred all those questions to the sheriff after her statement was completed.

Then she got into her plans for the money. "It was born of the most terrible war this country has ever known. Countless people died over this gold. One man, who was my ancestor, envisioned using it to alleviate suffering instead of inflicting it. For his good intentions, he lost his life at the hands of his own brother. I want to try and wipe out the evil that surrounded this treasure in the past. I want it to be used for the greatest good to the community." She paused for a moment and looked out at the crowd of faces listening in hushed silence for a moment.

"When I came here, this community was a refuge for me. I was running from an abusive marriage. My ex-husband didn't beat me physically like Zeke Folsome and his kind beat the 'Wanda's' and even worse, the 'Rose's', who cannot help themselves. Of course, that doesn't happen just here. It's all over, in the richest of homes as well as the poorest shack in the woods. That's one of the reasons why I am announcing the opening of the Donald Stuart Foundation. The foundation's main goal will be to offer training and support to abused wives and their children. The Jonathan Saunder's House will be constructed on the site of the old barn. It will provide temporary housing for women with no other refuge. It will have six spacious bedroom and bath apartments, with a large shared kitchen and dining room. Women and children could stay there while they were learning a trade that would help them remain independent of their abusers. Women who wanted to learn to be chefs would begin their training in the house kitchen and provide meals not only for the residents but for enrollees at the Louisa Murcott Institute."

A reporter interrupted, "What's the Louisa Murcott Institute?"

"That's the other reason I am doing this," Casey replied. "The other great tragedy I saw here was all of the wisdom and skills of the past being lost in our technological society. Our ancestors made everything they had. They made it with love and skills that are no longer accepted as valuable. Well, I want to make the wood carvers and the weavers and the potters and all of the other people that made this part of the world a special place important again. I want to give the old skills a rebirth. I want people to come to these mountains and not envision stereotypical ignorant 'hillbillies'. Instead I want them to see musicians, craftsmen and artisans who deserve a special place in history. My cabin is going to be the nucleus of it. Later, we plan to add several other buildings that will be representative of the nineteenth century village that existed here. The institute will teach the old skills like weaving and quilt making to women who want to earn a living as artisans. There is still a place for fine handmade items that cannot be duplicated by any machine-made counterparts. It will also teach office and administrative skills to the women who want to learn that. The institute is going to be a business and will need all the staff any other business will. Ms. Margaret MacDougal has consented to be the institute's director. She will say a few words after I finish." The group looked bewildered until someone noticed Miz Maggie standing in the background. Then a cheer went up among the older local residents, "That's Miz Maggie. Bless her heart."

Casey nodded. "Yes! Miz Maggie. One of the wisest women I have ever met. She's a fine artisan and will pass on not only her knowledge, but her pride in the old crafts."

Casey answered a lot of questions about the proposed foundation, then one reporter from Towns Count threw her a personal question. "What are you going to do now that Velma Lou is in jail and the Bluejay Bugle is temporarily shut down? Are you interested in getting on the staff of another local paper? Our paper is looking for a good reporter."

Casey shook her head and reached for Lee's hand. "I've got my work cut out for me. I'll be overseeing the foundation, getting married and having a family. And I'm going to write a book."

"What'cha gonna write about?" a voice shouted.

Casey replied, "Why, Bluejay. The way it was here a little over a hundred years ago and the people who made it what it is today.

Photo by Veronica Byrd-Mahameed

Kathleen is a travel writer and frequent contributor to publications, such as *Woodall's Publications, Family Motor Coaching, Doggone Newsletter* and *Georgia Backroads,* Other books by her include a novel, *Last Step,* and *Georgia's Ghostly Getaways,* a spirited travelog about the best haunted spots in Georgia.

She is currently working on *Finding Florida's Phantoms,* a ghostly guidebook to the sunshine state.

Kathleen lives high in the Georgia mountains in her cabin with her very own Smokey, Romeo, her canine companion and the latest addition to the family, Georgia, an abandoned tabby kitten.

She explains why she wrote *Kudzu,* the legends and the culture enthralled me. One day, while looking at a cabin almost engulfed by Kudzu, the idea for a novel that combined the physical beauty of the area with the history and culture was conceived. Kudzu evolved into a tale of love and betrayal, past and present, set against the backdrop of these ancient mountains."

Printed in the United States
25708LVS00001B/160-207